memorandum
from the iowa
cloud appreciation
society

memorandum from the iowa cloud appreciation society

A NOVEL

Joseph G. Peterson

University
of Iowa Press
Iowa City

University of Iowa Press, Iowa City 52242
Copyright © 2022 by Joseph G. Peterson
uipress.uiowa.edu
Printed in the United States of America

Cover design by Kathleen Lynch, Black Kat Design
Text design and typesetting by Omega Clay

Printed on acid-free paper

Library of Congress Cataloging-in-Publication Data
Names: Peterson, Joseph G., author.
Title: Memorandum from the Iowa Cloud Appreciation Society / Joseph G.
    Peterson.
Description: Iowa City: University of Iowa Press, [2022]
Identifiers: LCCN 2022004939 (print) | LCCN 2022004940 (ebook) | ISBN
    9781609388775 (paperback; acid-free paper) | ISBN 9781609388782 (ebook)
Subjects: LCGFT: Novels.
Classification: LCC PS3616.E84288 M46 2022 (print) | LCC PS3616.E84288
    (ebook) | DDC 813/.6—dc23/eng/20220224
LC record available at https://lccn.loc.gov/2022004939
LC ebook record available at https://lccn.loc.gov/2022004940

Yoga figure courtesy of Lily Peterson

To fellow friends and travelers:
Edward L. Shaughnessy and Sean Clark

Ziggurats of lightning tear through the dark sky,
The vaporous dome is shredded,
And rain falls in ribbons.
—memorandum from the Iowa Cloud Appreciation Society

Yet what was it to be out there
to be alone and among ourselves
the chatter of all our days unraveling
casual as birdsong . . .
—from the Wilderness Journal of Michel S. Tremblay

memorandum
from the iowa
    cloud appreciation
society

chapter 1
cumulus fractus

Travel was an ineluctable part of Jim Moore's life. It seemed he
was always in airports waiting for planes. His work demanded it. He
lived in Chicago, but his sales territory was the Southwest, Florida,
upstate New York—particularly Albany—and, on a more regular
basis than he wished, Cleveland.

Had his territory been consolidated into one locale or the other
he might have moved to reduce hours spent in the air, but because
his territory was split schizophrenically across the continent, and this
was due to the fact that his company was too cheap to hire adequate
staff to cover these territories, and because central headquarters
was located in Schaumburg, it made sense to live in Chicago.

His boss, the owner of the company, was fond of saying *First we
plan the attack, then we attack the plan.* Whatever analysis resulted from
such a proposition usually ended with Moore headed off in some
uncharted direction. You want more, Moore, his boss said, smiling
as he dropped his readers on his nose and removed the papers from
his desk, then strike out for the Southwest—I've been wanting to do
business there for years.

Moore, unwilling to say no—he was a natural-born salesman,
after all—merely said yes, he agreed: Yes, yes, it would be a fine idea,

Harvey, I think I will, and like that: Google Maps searched, airport schedules, car rentals, hotel reservations, and travel itineraries pieced together on the fly, he'd be off to another part of the country, conquering hitherto undiscovered territories for Harvey Sonnenshein & Sons.

He's the sunshine, Moore thought, *and I'm the bird that twirls in its splendor.*

Now Moore was pinned down in some northeastern airport because of snow—near-blizzard conditions. He looked around the gate watching his fellow travelers, trying to guess whom he might be sitting next to on the airplane. Early in his career Moore had enjoyed talking to the person he sat next to on the plane, but now with computers and the demands of work, combined with the ever-shrinking space allotted in the cramped quarters, he was happy to ignore those around him and work, or if not work, to try to catch up on sleep. His only request, really, was that whoever sat next to him on the plane didn't violate his personal space with a creeping arm on the armrest or a tilted body in sleep that would sometimes fall on his.

Off in the corner of the gate was a large man who was looking directly at Moore as if he was expecting Moore to get up and do something, but there was nothing to do but sit and wait for the planes to get going. The man was eating a Big Mac and sipping from an extra-large pop. *He's the guy I'll be forced to sit next to,* Moore thought. *I guarantee it.*

Though Moore liked his job—he often found himself agreeing, absurdly, that he loved it—he often felt that the pain of travel outweighed what pleasure he received from it. He never got over the sense that he was horribly ill-equipped for the ordeal of moving anonymously through large crowds in the airport. But then, who was so equipped? Pilots, he thought. Security guards . . . the minions, the barely noticed workers who plied their trade here. He supposed too that some of the better-traveled, and better-paid, business travelers could do it.

Moore was always amazed at how fluidly some of the other business professionals seemed to move through the crowds, unflappably good-natured, their crisp business outfits unruffled by the heave-ho of the crowd. The world was their oyster and they moved through it as such. There were also vacationers already dressed for the beach in flip-flops and flower-print shirts, who were headed off to better places—and who were so smitten by the allure of their tropical destination that the means of arrival barely registered on their consciousness.

Moore was altogether different. It was a consolation to think so, at least. He felt older than he was—and it was the travel that did it to him. Travel was that force, which, like the winds that blasted the face of the desert Sphinx, wore away at him. He often found himself wondering why he was squandering his better years in airports, between destinations, nowhere home. Worse, he worried that the stress of travel not to mention the loss and finding and loss again of his circadian rhythm did weird things to his thought processes.

He worried he would die younger than he should, worried about dying alone, unmoored, unmourned, lost. He tried his best to stay relaxed—he kept telling himself, even under the most trying conditions, to relax, remain calm.

Under the most stressful travel conditions, he had a habit of imagining some place far from the airport. Was it a form of dementia, he wondered, to do so? As he got older it became easier and easier to slip away into this imaginary place. It helped him release stress. Lately he had been imagining a Woodsman (*What is a Woodsman?* he wondered). The Woodsman had come to Moore one day in a dream and when the Woodsman indicated with a crooked finger that Moore follow, he couldn't resist. *Come along, Jim,* the Woodsman seemed to be saying. *Come. Follow me. I want to show you something.*

3

The Woodsman marched through a wild arboreal forest of ancient hemlock, he skirted the rocky shoals of a deep freshwater lake, and there in the distance on the side of a mountain was a log cabin with a little ribbon of smoke coming out of the stone chimney. Moore followed close behind, best he could, huffing and puffing. *Jesus*, he thought. *This is tough going.*

Moore didn't know exactly when the Woodsman lived or where, nor did he know what the Woodsman did to survive. What Moore did know, though, was that the Woodsman somehow or other lived an elemental existence, close to nature, far from crowds, far from the technology of the modern world. It was a good enough existence for Jim Moore as well and it made him happy deep in his heart's core that the Woodsman had made himself known to him.

Moore also doesn't know where the idea of this Woodsman came from. He may as well have come from an L.L.Bean catalog—not the internet version that the kids order from today, but the actual L.L.Bean catalogs that he had seen in his youth—stocked with dozens of varieties of boots with rubber lug soles and leather uppers with the felt liners. There were also the rugged black-and-red wool jackets that put him in mind of the north woods, and the yellow rain slickers that seemed designed for none less than sea captains hanging one hand from the wires staring into the salty sea spray of a nor'easter. And every clothes item was followed by a range of sizes and specifications with prices all rounded, oddly, to the quarter.

It wasn't that long ago such catalogs were available, but it was long enough ago from the present moment to make Jim say that things had been different then, or rather that things had definitely changed from then to now.

Well, how have they changed? he remembers one ex-girlfriend or another from his distant past asking him. Usually Moore can identify the feminine voice as some previous girlfriend (there had been a total of five) but more often than not it was an amalgam of all the girlfriends he had known—an average, the mean, or rather the best parts of each sifted out into some new imaginary woman that Moore was holding out for.

He understood the collective presence of these women as signposts directing the way toward where he must go to find the woman most suitable for him. Taken together, and analyzed, they formed some portrait of a type of woman not only whom Moore would desire but more importantly who would desire him—a person with whom, for the most part, Moore would be able to get along. Such a woman, once found, would offer counterargument to the opinions Moore liked to put forward.

Moore liked to have his ideas tested, and he regretted that he hadn't been successful in finding a woman—a soul mate, a partner, a spouse, an oppositor; whatever you want to call it—who cared enough about his ideas to put them to the test. *It's nice to have some sort of argument,* Moore thought, *just as long as it doesn't get out of control or lead to hand-to-hand combat.* No. He didn't want that to happen. All he wanted was a little resistance to his own wandering mind. *It keeps one honest,* he thought.

In response to her voice: *How have things changed from the days of your youth to now?* Well, there was only one response, particularly if he was willing to be absolutely honest with himself, and with her. They have changed for the worse. Why, look around this gate, for God's sake, all these people, rotting in their winter clothes, crowded together, hunkered down until the planes got moving again, if they'd get moving again: the storm out there showed no sign, presently, of abating. What a mess.

chapter 2
cumulus humilis

Yes, Moore hated to admit it—and he never thought he'd be the guy to say it, but it was true. Things had gone to hell. It wasn't that long ago the world seemed in a better place. Now, with the advent of personal technology and the deeply seductive tug of phones, laptops, computers, digital tablets, handheld games—devices that buzzed, beeped, ticked, glimmered, glowed, spoke, and answered, and now with the incredible ubiquity of such devices the world had taken, in Moore's opinion, a decidedly downward turn. We've gone from a mostly social society where we interact with one another in the three dimensions of the tangible unrecorded real to an onanistic one where our main interaction is with machines: glitzy glamorous machines no doubt, but machines nonetheless and the shouting clamorous voices and alluring digital souls that inhabit those machines grabbing and not letting go of our attention.

Why, if you need proof, just look at this young couple sprawled out on the bench next to him. Look at the way they comport themselves: they are oblivious to everyone around them, seemingly in love, but more to the point they are hoodwinked out of some sort of authentic interaction with each other by some poor simulacrum of it in the form of a phone.

6

And who knew what crap the kids these days were pumping into their ears through their earbuds. What were these kids doing to their ears? It was a form of madness to blow one's ears out before the age of twenty. What was going to happen in thirty years' time when a whole generation of kids raised on "devices" and sonically blinkered by earbuds or headphones went suddenly deaf and had to come up for air? And here you have, literally, a whole generation, perhaps an era of people who have escaped the noose of reality and who have gotten so lost in the hinterlands of social media and the internet that not one of them is able to find their way back to the real. That slippery thing identity, hard enough to hold on to even under the best of conditions, was now lost in a fun house of mirrors, a vast echo chamber of self. As they disappeared down the drain of the internet via the portal of these devices, Moore felt like one of the last persons standing looking around wondering why they all got up and left.

And who was going to take care of them when they needed taking care of? Moore thought. Not me, he mumbled—knowing, even as he said this, that it probably would be the likes of him—if he even lived that long. Moore knew that those who remained vigilant to reality proper—those like him who did so out of duty rather than nostalgia—would likely be the ones to hold down the fort when the shit hit the fan or rather when the internet went kaput because of some catastrophe and these others had to swim up out of Narcissus's pool, bewildered by daylight.

Moore tried to think positive thoughts but this waiting at the gate in an airport shut down by blizzard conditions gave him too much time to observe and reflect on humanity. What's more, the air at the gate, which seemed recirculated through an overloaded or faulty filtration system, stank, souring his view of the matter. *And it'll probably be worse on the plane*, which was likely to be dirty, claustrophobic, and musty—the condition they kept these birds in these days. *Thank God it's only a ninety-minute flight!*

chapter 3
cumulus mediocris

While Moore sat there, he kept looking over his shoulder at the young couple who were both long and skinny and not unlovely. They were alternately snapping selfies and broadcasting them, no doubt, out into the digital cloudscape of their own social network and there was something about this behavior that puzzled him. Who were they, Moore wondered—even as he was annoyed by their behavior with the phone and by the way they mistook the airport chairs for a sofa in their own dorm room? Then, as an afterthought, Moore wondered: *Am I jealous?* But jealous of what? Their youth? Their beauty? Their crazy hermetic relationship that broadcast itself to all, even as they remained, more than ever, drawn to themselves?

No, Moore wasn't jealous, far from it, he was happy he had long ago progressed beyond this period of life. *Let them have what they have,* he thought. *I'm happy with mine.*

Nevertheless, there were times Moore wished he could say he was young. Wouldn't it be wonderful to be like that boy again, sitting in an airport with an attractive girl, going somewhere far from home?

Sure, one ear was plugged into an earbud but the other ear was cocked to a future that, in all of its unexplored newness, beckoned!

That was the allure of youth, of venturing forth into the world for the first time: the whole future was spread out in front of you like a map filled with possibility and what wonder to be on the cusp of it all with a girl or with a friend right there next to you, sharing your earbud and waiting in the wings.

Oh, to be young, Moore thought. It all passed by so quickly. *If I knew then what I know now!*

Whenever Moore felt particularly blue about it, he liked to look at himself in the mirror. It had nothing to do with vanity. It was his way of correcting a wandering body image that drifted uncomfortably toward the old, the disheveled, the slightly overweight, and worst of all, the scowling.

At times Moore felt on the edge of death, not from any malign disease but from simply petering out. He looked in the mirror and smiled. No, he wasn't a scowler. His gums were good, a healthy pink, and his teeth had been orthodontically set. He had whitened his teeth only six months ago. He wanted to remove the stain of years of coffee drinking. What a difference whitening made, he thought. One who scowls doesn't go out of his way to whiten his teeth. Only someone cheerful would do such a thing.

Moore had exhorted himself throughout his life, in all sorts of situations, to smile. What's more, he knew the importance of having a relaxed, easygoing smile. His sales improved because of it, and he was certain he picked up friends as a result. *Only smile,* he would tell himself, *and the happiness that smiles portend will be yours.*

It seemed like a crazy, simple idea, foolish perhaps, but its simplicity was part of its charm. *The more I smile, the happier I feel,* he told himself. But often he didn't smile, and worse, he didn't feel all that happy. He couldn't help it. Beneath the happiness just described lay a substratum of sorrow that Moore couldn't account for—a deep primordial layer of woe stretching back eons through his DNA to some apelike melancholic ancestor who smashed his thumb while flinting an arrow, then let out a howl of grief that echoed through the countless generations until it had lodged itself in Moore's own heart like a festering sore: a sorrow that sometimes yielded tears but more and more often these days gave way to anger and rage.

As Moore aged, he discovered with some horror that the rage leaped out with reflexive speed (was this too a sign of incipient dementia?) and before he could correct himself he had either done or said something that he quickly regretted. It had even happened today.

Moore'd been standing in a long queue waiting to check in his bags. The skinny twentysomething man standing in line behind him and also cocooned from the world in large soft headphones kept vocalizing lyrics from a song that only he could hear. He threw up his hand and dropped it and threw it up again, gesturing to the song he was plugged into, and in the process he inadvertently bumped Moore with his forearm. At that point Moore turned around, his face flustered, and demanded loud enough so the youth would hear him through the headphones: "Would you give me some space, please!"

Moore had spoken loud enough so that other people in line heard him. They turned; they looked scornfully upon Moore and Moore was embarrassed. It had happened so quickly, this rage, and he had been unable to stop it. What's more, he stood there now in line with all these people and he looked like a politically incorrect monster because he had scolded a young person sensitized by a culture that taught them how to feel their victimhood. It was a classic clash of generations and Moore had initiated it by turning on the kid.

After apologizing loud enough for those around him to hear, Moore turned and mumbled: What the hell. He said it over and over again—as if the saying were a salve over a fresh wound of embarrassment and shame: What the hell. What the goddamned hell! Moore just stood there, smiling stupidly, and waited for his turn in line.

The problem was simple: Moore hated not being home. He hated traffic. He hated airports. He hated being in transition, always going from one place to another. He was always on the move, like one of those arctic terns that fly from one polar region to the other then back again, no rest but sleeping on the wind. *Though I move, my natural state, my deepest desire, is to remain still. Absolutely, and perfectly motionless.*

Moore admired people who had nowhere to go and nothing to do. When he ran into one of them on his journeys he would stupidly ask: *What's it like doing just nothing?* Only his genuine gawking kept the question from being an insult. Indeed, it was an insane thing to admire people locked to the geography of place and rendered inactive by circumstance, but admire them Moore did. He couldn't help it.

He fantasized continuously of leaving the glitz of all this technology behind and rocking one day on a rocking chair on some porch overlooking the mountains with absolutely nothing to do but rock forward and backward listening to the porch boards creak, watching the birds twitter in the high grass, and trying to reckon from the outline of the mountains and the shapes of the cumulus mediocris cloud formations some anthropomorphic partner or crowd of friends with whom he might commune.

Until that time, Moore was moving moving moving. No stopping, but always on the go.

chapter 4
cumulus congestus

Moore found himself checking his face in the mirror more and more often these days. He stood in the airport bathroom, washing his hands at the automatic tap after urinating. Men lingered longer in the bathroom now that all flights were grounded. He finished washing his hands and noticed himself in the mirror.

Seeing himself these days always slightly startled him. He was starting to bald. He noticed that the hair at the very top of his scalp was starting to disappear. It was during a business outing walking around the golf course playing a game of skins at the Imperial Country Club, situated in the palm-shrubbed outskirts of St. Petersburg, Florida, the blazing sun beating down, that Moore had been convinced of his hair loss: he woke in the morning with a blistering sunburn on the top of his pate. The sunburn was bad enough, but the loss of hair. It was a terrible blow.

Moore had liked his hair. He had kept it neatly cropped; he was very finicky about grooming. Always was. Nevertheless, when Moore discovered that his hair was starting to disappear on him, he wished that he had, as a youth (there's that word again!), grown his hair out in a wild mane.

Moore secretly loved how hair signified one's compliance or lack thereof with societal norms. He had always been a complier, hence his well-groomed head, but wouldn't it have been nice even for a summer between school years when no one was looking to grow his hair out: an unruly, curly mass—a flagrant fuck-you to the world of clocks and jobs and bosses? But he didn't have the courage. Moore had lacked courage for so many things. He saw it more and more the older he got.

If only I'd had more courage as a kid, I might have met the woman of my dreams. I might even have had the career of my dreams. As it is, I sat on the sidelines most of my life. Moore remembers school dances, always the wallflower. What would it have taken to step on the dance floor while the music was playing?

Moore realized more and more these days that he was a man of losses, not gains.

But he likes to point out from time to time that it was by being who he was that had gotten him this far. Moore was, by all accounts, an exceptional salesman. His company amply rewarded him for his hard-won service. What's more, he didn't complain. Instead, he tried to be ever hungry like a shark. *Give me more territory if you want*, he remembers telling his boss. *I can handle anything you throw at me.*

Then handle this, Harvey Sonnenshein said, giving him a map of the Southwest. *See what you can do with this territory!* And so, by leaps and bounds, Moore's territory had expanded into a vast though not very profitable network that nearly covered the entire continental United States of America.

Moore took his job seriously because, he reasoned, the more seriously you take it, the more important it becomes. He did research. He pored over his books for leads. He followed up every lead with a note—he was a meticulous note-taker (*the stories these notes alone could tell*, he thought from time to time, as he went over them), and he followed every note with a call. If a call led to a meeting, then he made time for the meeting. If the place to meet was in territory he had not yet broken into, he booked tickets and fixed his itinerary accordingly, and he dreamed on the flight over of the prospect of adding yet new quadrants to his sales territory. He would make money for Harvey Sonnenshein yet. Just be patient, give him time. He was hungry, like a shark.

chapter 5
stratocumulus castellanus

Moore sat looking out the window at the blizzard—it was a complete whiteout—and at the crowded gate: too many faces to register. He closed his eyes, then let them open again. *What is a Woodsman?* Moore asked himself. He imagined wandering around an ancient forest with colossal trees that stretched unbelievably toward a crown of craggy branches and needles. Moore wanted to be in such a far-off imaginary place so far distant from the current complexities of modern life. What a thing . . . to be there!

Moore remembers reading of the micro-biosphere that existed high up in the redwood forests. The tops of the ancient trees were so huge and far removed from earth, capturing the clouds as they drifted by, that they had their own climate and specialized fauna that had adapted to living in the upper branches.

Scientists had even figured out a way to harness themselves on ropes and ratchet themselves high up into the boughs of the great trees, and there they stayed for days on end making careful analysis of what lived in the upper branches: exotic species of bumblebees, and beetles and larvae, and other bugs and plants both small and exceedingly large.

Moore liked that word, "larvae," by the way, and what it suggested: a white, sticky, and blind worm so stuffed with life that it wiggled.

These ideas from science that Moore had gleaned from newspaper articles and *National Geographic* got mixed in with mythic images garnered from childhood reading and from early Disney features so that Moore imagined that the lightning-blasted tree crowns, hollowed out, were moss-filled with such luxurious and green-tufted splendidness that they seemed the very bed ready-made for a disappeared race of giants who spoke some variant of fee-fie-fo-fum.

The woods of Moore's imagination were so mist-saturated and rain-soaked that beams of light seldom penetrated the forest bottoms to illuminate the ferns and animal creatures below. And what creatures occupied the forest bottoms? Bears, deer, red fox, and flying squirrels, perhaps, and perhaps the gnomic woodsmen who were all-knowing of the woods but knew nothing else beyond the universe of the woods.

In his happiest dreams, this was what Moore wanted: a green-saturated and arboreal life of shadow and flickering darkness. We come from the trees, Moore reasoned, and some part of us wants to return to the trees.

But now, unfortunately, it wasn't so easy to do: the great forests were being chopped down and with global warming there was the apocalyptic horror of watching them go up in flames. Moore didn't expect they would even outlast his own mortal life. What nature spent eons making, we spent a generation or two destroying and converting to housing sites and cul-de-sac tract suburbs and iterative big-box strip malls that not only stretched as far as the eye could see but obliviated whatever wilderness, redwood, prairie, swamp, or otherwise that got in the way of their cancerous growth.

Isn't it clear enough, Moore thought, that things had taken a turn for the worse? It was an act—this savaging of the wilderness—that, sooner or later, we would pay for. Though the woods bore the loss silently, the deeper wisdom that all this would tilt against humankind remained.

Moore wished in his heart of hearts that he had someone with whom to share this observation. He looked around at the faces of the people at the gate and they were all strangers: as indifferent to him as he was to them. Humanity, en masse, especially those gathered in airports, always concerned him. Growing surging crowds and the expanding unchecked growth of the human population that they represented had the effect of making his own life seem of diminishing consequence. *It's the principle of the individual*, he liked to say, *that always gets torn asunder in a crowd.*

Moore liked the sound of that word, "asunder," and he used it from time to time to good effect. The sight of all these people made him feel less and less a singularity and more a sample of an endlessly repeating type: *Homo sapiens.*

chapter 6
stratocumulus lenticularis

Moore stared at one television screen, which broadcast the weather. The weather had been bad all day and it was only getting worse. Doppler radar proved that. TVs set up in the terminal had broadcasters panning to different locations buried under snow from the Midwest through the Northeast. There were shots of snowplows bailing out in Topeka, which was a territory of Moore's that he would be flying to in a week.

Eau Claire, Wisconsin, was said to have received twenty-eight inches of snow in the last twenty-four hours, and in New Hampshire along Interstate 93, just north of Manchester, there was a twenty-five-car pileup caused by icy roads and low visibility. A truck was jackknifed, the trailer split when it hit a roadside tree: the trucker was thrown from his cab and landed twenty feet away headfirst in a snowdrift. A local hookup was sending video footage of emergency vehicles untangling the tragic mess.

The large storm system, a bomb cyclone, was caused by a confluence of bitter cold from the north and a storm system in the Gulf that had trekked north, bringing warm wet air in tumescent clouds, and the size of the monster storm was said to be the result of vast energy systems brought on by global warming. The meteorologist in a red dress, with hollowed-out cheeks, large eyes, and an incredibly large mouth used touch screen weather maps, satellite images, and those live feeds to show exactly what was happening.

Moore watched, alternately beguiled by her face and by the satellite images that showed the large swirling cloud system from the Gulf, and arrows pointing down from Canada demonstrating the arctic chill that was coming down. As she talked, the sound of the TV blotted out by the ambient noise of the airport, a crawl of words deciphering what she said moved across the bottom of the screen.

He couldn't hear a word of what she was saying and he didn't care to read it—although he knew it couldn't bode well for him. Nevertheless, he was able to watch her move her mouth and it made him wonder about the strange exaggerated human faces with their gaping smiles television producers sought to put forth on TV, and this broadcaster here with her skeletal jawbone and ring-haunted eyes and surprisingly fulsome breasts hinted at by a low-cut blouse was just striking enough to make Moore want to keep watching, while the weather, the terrible winter, wreaked havoc on the world just outside the window.

chapter 7
stratocumulus stratiformis

Moore sat there now, slumped in his chair. He felt a wreck. He looked around at his fellow travelers, many of whom were still in galoshes and cocooned in their winter coats. Luggage filled the space. Pushed up against his chair, so that it was almost touching, was an airport luggage cart—and three or four more carts were scattered at the gate. Nearby too was a garbage can filled to the top with trash. On the floor, underneath the chair across from him, lay scattered abandoned newspapers left by someone who had departed into the snow-filled sky on the last flight out.

The marooned were left sitting at the gate watching the news or eating fast food, or working on their computers, or listening to their iPods, or talking on their cell phones, or they were typing rapidly into their handhelds or digital tablets or electronic readers that were in Moore's humble opinion a poor substitute for actual face-to-face conversation. Moore occasionally tried to express this opinion to colleagues of his, but no one was listening to him because they were busy texting.

Others were hunched over a laptop typing or they were curled around tablets streaming movies and accessing any number of game-oriented apps. The world had gone toward the technological, that much was clear. It had left the life of the Woodsman behind just as surely as the city had left the dark night behind when the streets became lit with the orange luminescence emitted from high-pressure sodium lighting.

But I want to be a Woodsman, Moore thought. I want to live wild, close to the earth in a hovel. I want a simpler life, he thought. This traveling wore him out. It made him feel disconnected. When he returned to Chicago he was going to ask Harvey to consolidate his territory so he could bring this traveling under control. It was something he had been contemplating for years, but perhaps now was the time to make the move, time to consolidate, time to stay in one place, time to start focusing on some of the other things life had to offer.

Like what, Moore thought, a moment later. What else would I do with my life? What would I do with more free time? The nice thing about all this traveling, it keeps me occupied, but with more free time, who knows what might happen? Why, anything could happen, and if I don't ask for more free time now, then when? And if I don't do it soon, is all of this traveling really sustainable? It's wearing me down. I'll talk to Harvey about it next week. The far West would work for me, or the East Coast, or, for that matter, the Midwest—drivable from the city. Just no more airport terminals.

Moore had vowed to ask for consolidation in the past, but whenever he tried to ask for it, as if sensing what Moore was going to ask, Harvey Sonnenshein held out a lead as bait to keep him going. I have a handful of leads here, Jim, that should interest you seeing as they would help you expand your territory some. And the problem was, Moore couldn't resist Harvey's cunning offer. Whenever the opportunity presented itself to hit new territory he was the first to volunteer, and whenever Harvey asked how he was holding up, he couldn't help but say, as enthusiastically as possible: Things are going excellently, Harvey. No complaints. The only complaint is that my customers don't come in for bigger buys, but what I don't get in buys, I'm happy to make up for in volume. Do you have any leads? I'm heading to the Pacific Northwest for the week and *after that, I'm headed to L.A. Any leads you have to grow this thing would be much appreciated.*

Moore closed his eyes and tried to imagine the Woodsman. It's hard as hell with all the noise at the gate but he does his best. There the Woodsman stands in the shadows of a huge tree. Behind the Woodsman are the jagged contours of a snow-covered mountain. It was an image directly out of a beer commercial, but it was a place to start. *Hamm's, from the land of sky-blue wa-aters,* the jingle, which dated back to Moore's childhood, flowed into his brain, and then he switched back to the Woodsman. *That's the way to be,* Moore thought: a Woodsman comfortable in the untrammeled wilderness; a Woodsman who emerged into his own only while in the woods.

The problem with this life unlived away from the wilderness is that life has no scale to match itself against. Contemporary life was matched neither against the eons of time reflected back down from the stars nor from the modest hovel that shrank to obscurity against the mountain backdrop, nor from the shape of a human rendered tiny opposite the colossal forest. Instead, this life of ours was matched against the passing moment, against some bland sky-scrapers, and it was matched against the flickering digital images that, though ubiquitous, were nevertheless more evanescent than a fragile mayfly that gave up its life for a fleeting sexual encounter.

Worse still, Moore matched the success and merit of his own life against the sales figures of his competitors in the field, and by his position in the hierarchy of the Sonnenshein organization. Moore instinctively hated to lose ground to new hires, and he was always trying to outsell the strongest members from the old guard. *Sell,* Moore thought. *Sell, sell, sell and you will be well.* It was a mantra of his that he fervently believed. If he could only sell, and sell more, then everything would be all right.

22

Sales calls required that Moore be polite and a touch obsequious. He was always called upon to smile, to radiate calm, optimism, and happiness, but in his heart he was none of these things. A thick line ran vertically from his forehead and creased on the left side of his nose right near his eye, and it reflected the worry line of a perpetually knit and concerned brow. A permanent crease ran along his upper lip downward toward an at-times-disapproving and mildly jowly chin.

Hamm's, from the land of sky-blue wa-aters. Moore wished he had more imagination for this sort of thing. A lack of imagination was probably one of his greatest weaknesses. *I try to think more broadly, but I'm always brought back to the advertising jingle. I'm a natural salesman, after all. Hamm's, from the land of sky-blue wa-aters.* Now that it was in his ear, he couldn't get the jingle out. It was not of the moment but of all time. The jingle would outlast the trees.

chapter 8
stratus fractus

As for how the rest of Moore was holding up, well, quite truthfully, he felt worn out. His lower back never seemed to align anymore. When he woke in the morning, he had to carefully roll out of bed so as not to further damage his already weakened spine. And what had weakened it? Why, sitting in these damned airports, and hunched over, crouched down in the uncomfortable airline seats.

Toting his heavy bags, and always carrying an overloaded satchel, also wore away at him. Moore's shoulder was stiff, and he was starting to feel arthritis in his joints, particularly in his wrists, and this in turn seemed to weaken his grip. When he reached for handholds now, they often slipped right out of his grasp, and when shaking a client's hand, he often felt outmatched: the strength of their grip pitted against the weakness of his. Handshakes had become a silent moment of embarrassment to Moore for just this reason. He noticed, too, one day last summer, while playing a pickup softball game with clients, that he no longer possessed the flexibility and limberness of his youth. He attempted to slide into second base. As a kid Moore was an expert slider, but as an adult, the movement of his lower body as he attempted, leg first, to go prone, caused him flinching pain and he was so physically awkward while he slid that teammates of his laughed and jeered from the dugout and he would have been called out if the second baseman, equally awkward, hadn't dropped the ball. It only highlighted that his body was stiffening and getting brittle with age. This growing old was a terrible calamity and in truth, Moore wasn't ready for it.

Moore was trying to remember being young, though he couldn't remember why he was trying to do so. Then he saw the young couple that was still lying across the chairs listening to their handhelds and they alternated typing on them with their thumbs and occasionally they snapped selfies while they lay entwined in the molt of their winter clothes on the airport floor. He tried to jog his memory. *What was I like then, when I was their age: when the world seemed larger and I was still unknown to myself?* He dwelled on this thought a moment, then let it pass.

chapter 9
stratus nebulosus

Moore stared across the gate at the heavy man stuffing his face with French fries. Now the man was eating a Big Mac. Moore could smell the Big Mac from where he sat—smell the slightly sweet, slightly sour smell of the "special sauce" commingled with the greasy smell of the burger and the fries. Moore had long ago given up McDonald's, and he was often fond of saying *If I were alone on a desert island and all there was for food was a McDonald's restaurant then I'd happily starve or eat the raw seafood that washed up on the beach.* That being said, the jingle *Two all-beef patties* had lodged itself into Moore's brain years ago and even now he couldn't see a Big Mac without quietly, almost against his will, singing the jingle. *How is it possible,* Moore thought, *after all these years—how many has it been? Thirty? Thirty-five years? I can still remember that jingle but so much else from that time of my life: the warmth of my mother's body, the look of my childhood bedroom, the feel of having my whole life ahead of me—all these things have vanished completely from my memory. I can't even recall the sound of my father's voice.*

The man eating the Big Mac was unbelievably heavy, though at first glance one didn't appreciate his true immensity. Moore looked and wondered what it was that kept a person from grasping how vast some truly heavy people were—on first glance? Was it the way they wore their clothes? Their posture, an inherent grace, or was it the way the mind was set: to expect humans to fall within a certain range of sizes—and if the person in question exceeded this range the brain automatically registered the person as smaller than they were?

It was a question for psychologists, perhaps, Moore thought. In any event the man eating the Big Mac was even larger than Moore had at first thought. The man was jowly, with excess flesh hanging loose beneath the jaw hinge. His cheeks were puffy, slightly rosy. They glistened imperceptibly beneath a layer of sweat. The man took long slow bites at the hamburger. With surprising daintiness and care, he nibbled the fries—as a small mammal might. He ate and enjoyed the hamburger and made it seem a larger, more expansive meal than it was.

I have never seen a human nibble McDonald's fries so carefully, Moore thought. After each French fry the man licked his finger, picked up another fry, and dipped it in ketchup, which he'd squirted into the top of his Big Mac container. He proceeded to nibble it carefully. He slowly stuffed the fry into his mouth. Again, the fat man licked his fingers, picked up his napkin and wiped the corner of his mouth and he tapped dry the beads of sweat forming on his temple. The man paused a moment, then reached over and grabbed the large soda pop and sucked thoughtfully from the straw. The man set the pop aside and quietly belched. The man paused as if ruminating over something. After a moment, he picked up the Big Mac and took another bite. He chewed the bite carefully as if savoring the flavor, or—was he trying to maximally extract nourishment from the burger, letting his saliva do as much of the digesting as possible? A swallow. A pause. A reach for a fry. Dip. Nibble. Dip. Nibble. Wipe. Pause. Sip. Belch. Repeat.

It was probably an addiction to McDonald's that was responsible for the man's heft. Yet Moore identified with the man. He couldn't help it. Everywhere Moore looked he felt somehow as if he saw a reflection of himself. And it wasn't a very nice reflection. It only depressed him. *These crowds*, he thought, *will do that to you.*

chapter 10
stratus opacus

Moore felt old and shabby, all of a sudden—as if his own moment of youth had left him so long ago that he could barely remember what it was like while he was in the middle of it.

Perhaps, he thought, a moment later, *this is why I'm unable to understand the youth of today. Oh look at me,* he thought, *I'm already referring to these kids as the "youth of today." I was young once and it wasn't that long ago. I used to hate it when my elders used that expression around me: "the youth of today." What kind of phrase is that?* he wondered. *The youth of today. It sounds like a rock band—and not a very good one at that. And this word, "elders," is that what I am? What I've become? An elder?*

But this youth is different, Moore thought. *They are technologically plugged in in a way that I and my generation—graduating high school class of 1983—have never been plugged in. What does it all mean to be hyper-plugged-in? Switching between phone calls, emails, texts, social media, the reality of the street, and the reality of the computer screen?*

Last week, as a matter of fact, Moore almost ran someone over who was crossing the street while texting on her cell phone. He was in Cleveland driving a rental car down to the bottom of a hill on Edgehill Drive. The road ahead had a bend in it and as Moore came through the bend into the intersection, which had a green light, a woman ambled into the road. The woman hadn't even bothered to lift her head to check and see if oncoming traffic was rushing through the intersection. He honked, *beep beep*, swerved, and barely missed her—he felt like a bowling ball hooking at the last minute just missing the pin.

As Moore passed her by, he checked his rearview mirror to see if she was wobbled, thrown off her balance—or if her attention was at least momentarily diverted from her electronic device. As it was she hadn't even lifted her head from her phone, her thumbs typing into it. This inexplicably angered Moore. *She's safe, unscathed by me, and yet she's an automaton wandering the streets absorbed by a virtual world but ignoring the one that could kill her.* It would serve her well if she had been hit, wake her up. Only Moore didn't want to be the one to do it.

That was it, Moore thought. The problem with it all. People so plugged into alternate realities that they no longer believe in or take seriously the reality they physically inhabit for better or worse. People always switching, what do they call it?—multitasking—never staying in the same mode for long. Sentences broken midconversation, eye contact snapped and the intimate human moment lost as the head is lifted to the television set in the corner or dropped to the digital device—and in this case what becomes of human connection?

It was a legitimate question, Moore thought. How come no one was asking it? Moore read the papers. He watched the news. In two different corners of the gate he saw it now: CNN was being broadcast in one corner; Fox News in the other. Cable TV personalities; talking heads were going at it without cease. Who were these people who spent their adult life in front of a camera and who seemed to have no private life, having given up private life in order to broadcast themselves into the vast global networks of information—and the evidence of multitasking was everywhere present on the TV screen. The perspective constantly shifted between the news anchor and the

30

anchor's simulacrum while a crawl of other news and information scrolled along the bottom of the screen.

It was a mode of being: addled by technology and surfeited by information, switching back and forth between conversations but never stopping to find the stillness. Everyone seemed to have fallen down the same rabbit hole together; everyone was entranced by this technology but very few people seemed to be asking the important question: is this really how we want to live?

It wasn't attention disorder, Moore'd been assured time and again, but assured by whom? Why, by clients, customers, friends, former girlfriends who grew tired of his complaining, and by these selfsame news anchors on the television screen that kept him and others including a whole generation of aging retirees addled through their golden years. All of these people had presented at one moment or another a calm voice of reassurance to Moore's complaint. This technology is a good thing, they argued. This new generation with their attention-grabbing gadgets: what these kids are suffering—and the whole population seemed to be suffering all of a sudden—is a disengagement from the real world, a moving away from face-to-face communication, a new mode of involvement made possible by a cursor and an illuminated screen and other handheld gadgets: this was not a bad thing at all, Moore had been assured, but a positive: a wonderful thing.

The world, after all, was vast and needed more than ever to be described: to be packaged and delivered. When one tired of watching talking heads describe the ravages across the land, one was able to turn inward and get lost in the distractions that technology had to offer.

In itself it was like a form of prayer, of engaged contemplation, even the posture of the head lowered toward the hands, which seemed folded in prayer but held instead the magical device, suggested as much. One person had even quipped that the human brain was made for this sort of digital multitasking, so it stands to reason that sooner or later it would create the reality it craved.

Nevertheless, it would all lead to no good. Moore was certain of it. He couldn't get Nietzsche's idea of religion out of his head. Nietzsche had called Christianity the "opiate of the masses," but technology had replaced Christianity and it was now the new opium. It was the new serum applied to the fatted calf to ready it for sacrifice. We will all be sacrificed and happily on the altar of technology, and then off with our heads before we even know what's coming.

But what did that mean? Off with our heads? Was technology really going to lead to the "offing" of our heads? Surely so, Moore thought: offing in the sense not of being lopped off, but rather of being turned off. Technology, Moore worried, was turning us off from each other. Worst of all, it was turning us off from ourselves.

Instead of rocking in the chairs listening to the porch boards squeak while reckoning friends in the shape of the hills beyond or in the passing clouds and trying to catch a wayward thought or memory—a cognition of our own—whole populations now sat entranced by one form of the tube or another.

Moore was convinced, and he would go to the mat with anyone who cared to argue the point, that all of this technology was creating in us a certain deafness to our own internal hum. Many no longer know it's there inside their own head: the unstoppable whisper that talks even while no one is listening, and the listening that no longer listens or hears the whisper that is conjured continuously from some mysterious, inscrutable abyss from within.

As a result, Moore was on hiatus from technology. It was his only form of revolt. He wasn't the only one. He was positive there were others like him and perhaps one day there would be a backlash—

and whole groups would pop up averse to the use of personal technology in public places.

Sure, while Moore worked, he would use the technology as he needed to, but while he traveled, he liked to travel perfectly unencumbered by electronic gadgets. *Better to observe the world rushing by while I'm on this side of the dirt to observe,* Moore thought, *than to disappear down some rabbit hole of technology only to end up at the end of the line wondering what I've missed.*

His only thought was to observe the world, and when he was too tired to observe, to let his own mind drone on to the cadence of its own interior hum.

Oh my, he thought, then yawned. A moment later he dropped off to sleep and a moment after that he was dreaming of the Woodsman.

chapter 11
stratus translucidus

It was morning when the Woodsman stepped out of his hovel. He wielded a large axe. He also had a longbow that required incredible strength to pull it back. The Woodsman, living close to the earth, pulled the bow with the greatest of ease and shot a buck. Later he gutted the buck with a bowie knife and strung it up by its hind legs to let it bleed. It felt good to acquire what one needed for food in such a rudimentary way.

The Woodsman's hovel was made of pine logs that he had set. First he had chopped the logs down with an axe. He had plundered the virgin forest for his timber. The trees that he chopped down had grown for centuries in virgin soil and he knew the lumber was of superior quality, filled with sap that would harden like resin over time.

He had hauled the logs out of the ancient forest by hitching them to a couple of mules. When he reached the river, he created a raft of the logs and floated them downstream to the site where he was to build his cabin. The site was on high ground, near a lake. A small stream flowed a hundred yards downhill of him. He was very happy with the site. He knew he would be able to fetch water but never be in fear of flooding. How lucky, he thought, to find such a place.

The Woodsman had cleared the site of trees and brush and packed the soil by making his mule team drag a heavy log back and forth on the site, applying pressure to the soil. He had no help in this, and he came naturally into understanding how to do this work. It was good work.

In the wilderness the Woodsman was plagued by the wildest and most mysterious dreams. He thought the dreams were slowly turning him into a saint.

In the morning with the sun up he laughed at the thought. He loved women too much to be a saint. Besides that, he didn't believe in God. He only believed in the truth of the wilderness, which said: we live only for a moment and then we die. Nothing cares that we lived. Nothing cares that we died.

The Woodsman hewed the logs of branches with a broad axe and an adze. He chopped out the notches and saddles at the ends of the logs, leaving a foot or so on either end for the sills. There was plenty of work to do and it was good work. He drank from the stream with a tin cup or with his hands, which were caked with dirt and tree sap. One of his fingernails had been mashed that morning and it still painfully throbbed. Off in the distance above the mountains rose the snow-capped mountain that gave the Woodsman comfort. He didn't know why the mountain comforted him, but in this land, all alone, it was like a friend to him. It was someone he could count on. He even found himself addressing the mountain in the first person.

Hey hill, he liked to say. How do you like the house I am building in your shadow? How is the snow up there? Are the mountain sheep summering on your high pastures?

35

In the autumn the sheep would come down from the mountain and the Woodsman would shoot them with his longbow in view of his cabin. It was nice to take them this way, he thought. *There is no difficulty in packing them out of here.* He hung the carcasses out on posts, salted and drying in the sun. In the evening he stored them high up in the trees to protect against bears.

In the evenings that followed during the summer he built his cabin, he piled the branches from the pine and burned them. The smell of pine was thick in the air and the sap cracked and popped in the heat of the fire.

The cabin he built was twenty feet by eighteen feet, perfectly suitable for his needs. He set it so it was true to the compass. The longer walls faced east and west with windows on either side. The door and one of the windows faced south to let in the light and the air. Opposite the door was a stone fireplace he built from granite stones pulled out of the stream that fed the lake. They were heavy but he carried each one of them up the hill from the stream by himself. *It is my time to live,* the Woodsman thought. *I will be dead soon enough. It's good to work.*

The Woodsman laid the logs one on top of the other, alternating the direction of the thick end of the log, and within a week he had built the walls of his cabin. They were eight logs high. He tapered the north and south walls to a point and carefully set the logs across the ends to form the roof joists. He elevated the heavy joists by using straps hooked to the mules and while they pulled, the logs rolled up a ramp he built for that purpose. When he was through with the structure, he thatched the roof and mortared the joints between the logs with a dirt-and-grass mixture.

While he worked he thought of his home life back on the farm in Iowa where he lost both of his parents one winter to illness. He nearly succumbed too, and lost part of his hearing from a prolonged fever. As it was, he had two white spots on his two front teeth that glowed like blind eyes against the yellowed ivory of his teeth.

The Woodsman's parents had been subsistence farmers and after they died he had to scrape to survive. He came north in search of work. The forests awaited and in the cities wood was needed. He headed to Canada. Lac du Bois. He settled in a small village near Sioux Narrows. He hooked up with a French-Canadian named Michel Tremblay, who was a logger and who helped the Woodsman get a job with the lumber company. Tremblay spoke in a dialect and it took all of the Woodsman's patience to make sense of what the Frenchman said. But he wouldn't miss it for anything in the world.

Do you work here?

Yes yes, skinnay, the Frenchman said, looking him over. And who else do you think works this madness called spinning the logs? And chopping them down? And rafting them together and running them down the river? No one but a crazy man will work on the boom and I been doing it more summers than I can count and still I'm alive, knock wood.

And how do I get a job on the boom? the Woodsman asked.

Can you stand on the log without falling down in the water?

Yes. I think I can. If it's tied on both ends.

The Frenchman laughed. Hokay, my friend, I suppose we'll see soon enough, but if you say so. I guess we can use you. Go on down on de stream where de water ain't so deep, an' tell Alfonse I sent you there and he'll set you up if you still want the job.

The Woodsman looked down where Michel Tremblay indicated. Over there?

You go on over there by that man with the pick-pole. Don't be scared. Alfonse will set you up on de last joint of the first beat and we'll watch how you do. Those hemlocks don't run so fast today in the shallows. Don't you worry, Alfonse will show you how to raft the logs together with hemp and by and by I betcha you can do him just as well as anybody else. Strong faller like you will be okay around

37

here. Just try not to fall in the water because if you do you may not come up for air, you understand?

The Woodsman nodded. Of course he understood. What other choice did he have? He needed a job this far north and if listening to the broken English of this crazy French Canadian was how he got his job, well then it was all the same to him. With that he was hired on the spot.

The Woodsman found rather quickly that he had the right body for this sort of work. It felt strange to be this lucky—that he found the exact work he was built for. It made him wonder if there weren't other loggers in his family's past. How else to explain it? He had been blessed with quick reflexes, physical intelligence, and a low center of gravity that helped him stay on top of the logs.

Michel Tremblay himself had nicknamed the Woodsman "Water Spider" for his seeming ability to straddle water and not fall through. The Woodsman learned to like the work and in the evenings he lay in a small cabin with the other men listening to them snore on the bunks.

He'd lie there and think of everything that happened to him during the day and he made plans to be better the next day: more physical, more agile, to work smarter, to get more done safely. Always stay on top of the logs, the Woodsman exhorted himself. No matter how fast and furious they come, keep your eyes open and your feet spinning on the logs this side of the water. By the end of the summer he was the foreman.

Michel Tremblay was so intent on keeping the Woodsman, he made him a twenty-five percent owner in the company.

In the early autumn, as they prepared for the winter cut, the Woodsman met a woman named Holly. He had just received his paycheck for the summer and wandered into town for a meal. He

38

stopped into a restaurant that was named, appropriately, The Lawg Caybun.

He sat down to eat. She served him moose meat and a stack of pancakes. When he ordered beer, she brought him beer. When he ordered schnapps, she brought him schnapps and smiled. His dog—a mutt with more Labrador retriever than anything else—guarded the door.

Earlier that day, the Woodsman had watched his dog attempt to hump a coyote in heat that had come down from the mountain, tail between her legs. The dog and coyote rubbed muzzles, and the dog attempted to mount the coyote. The Woodsman had seen it happening, but a noise—a bald eagle splashing into the lake for a perch—spooked the coyote, and what had started ended just as suddenly. The Woodsman actually felt sorry for his dog at the missed opportunity.

After the Woodsman had a shot of schnapps, he pushed his money onto the table. She collected his money, counted it up, grabbed his hand, and walked him upstairs to a room, swaying her ass as she went. It was the nicest room he had slept in since he left his parents' home years earlier. Her bed had springs, and as he lay in the bed, memories of his boyhood home flooded his mind. He'd been chopping trees, running them down the rivers, living on wild meat for so long he forgot that once upon a time long ago he had slept on a box mattress with bedsprings.

She pulled off his boots, which had twelve or so eyelets running up either side. They were strung together with leather laces.

You smell like pine cones, she said. And just as rough, too.

She pulled his socks off and massaged his feet, pushing her thumb and forefinger deep into the sensitive tissue near the balls of his feet. She found pain the Woodsman didn't know he had and tended to it. She removed his pants and started working on his calves, which were tense with muscle and hadn't been touched by another hand, including his own, in what seemed like years. He thought he would faint with pleasure. She worked both sides of his thighs, top and bottom, with her good strong hands rubbing all the sorrow and pain that had accumulated in them from being alone so long by themselves untended.

She massaged his back, stepping on him and balancing as a logger balances on a rolling log in the river. He laughed at the thought, as did she when he told it to her. Her arms were out at her side balancing akimbo as she carefully moved to and fro on his back, getting with her feet the nerves in his deep tissue that had been too long deprived of human touch and consideration.

When she was done stepping on him, she grabbed his forearms, which were corded with muscle, and she began massaging them. She moved to his calloused hands and mused at the strength of his fingers. They alone could crush her if they so desired, she said.

She removed her dress, and the frilly slip, and pulled her under-drawers, which were made of silk, off her bottom. She was a large, mottled, and round woman; a rash radiated from her neck to the upper part of her chest. Her cheeks too, were filled with blushing red.

When she moved, she jiggled. He reached out and touched her flesh and she was the softest person he had ever remembered touch-ing. His own body had been brutalized by too much hard work and there wasn't a spare piece of flesh on him. Her body by contrast was warm, soft, gentle. He felt, as a result, as if he had left the wilder-ness behind and entered a more civilized place.

She moved with spunk and good humor and laughed easily. She smelled of slightly sour milk, but behind that smell was a whiff of fresh bread mingled with the smell of earth and the lovely slightly perfumed odor of the crenellated mushrooms that his dog, Britt, liked to root out of the forest floor. It reminded him, more than any-thing, of mysterious life.

40

There was nothing mysterious about her actions, though, and yet he felt mystified nevertheless. She stroked him with her hand and a moment later she put him inside her. She started to move, at first slowly, then more quickly up and down on him. She pressed her hands into his chest, which was covered with dark curly hair. She rocked back and forth, the sweat breaking in tiny droplets from her forehead as if she had been cooking, instead, over a hot griddle.

The bed squeaked beneath them. She was filled with lust and sport. She was hot inside: hotter than bacon grease. He worried he might crack under her blows, but he held like a good piece of timber. She guffawed and pounded. At one point she slipped off him and before she could get back on, he shot his wad clean across the room. It hit the wallpaper on the opposing wall one foot below the ceiling.

He thought nothing of it. She got back on and continued. It occurred to him that he would probably tell Britt all about it on the walk back home.

Hiyya, she screamed, when he withdrew a second time. Whatcha doin', black scout! She slapped him hard in the face. It felt good to be slapped in the face, his teeth cutting the inside of his cheek so that he tasted blood. She tried to get back on but he pushed her away and on second thought he returned the clout to her face for good measure. He roughed her up more than he intended, the redness already coming to her cheekbone where his fist smacked. She was right, he could snap her in two with just his fingers. But he didn't. He wanted to keep her for more later after he got paid next season.

When the Woodsman left, his semen was still dripping down the wall. He noticed it was burgundy wallpaper with large velvet heart-shaped patterns. His semen had shot smack-dab in the middle of one of those hearts. He always was a good aim, he thought with a bit of lusty pride. He was still adjusting his suspenders. She cursed

41

him for messing the place up, then pushed him out and slammed the door behind him. Was that a smile? he wondered. Did she smile at him one last time before he was gone?

The way her tits swang all heavy, boy, you would have been proud of me. I was a hell of a sight better than you were today and that coyote you tried to hump before it was all scared away. And I don't blame her, the way you are—even wilder than a wild coyote. Well good for us, ole boy. One of us got it tonight. That should hold us until the end of winter provided we two survive that long.

It was a comparatively long monologue to which the dog merely panted and barked.

chapter 12
stratus undulatus

Adidas was a German shoe company, Moore remembered. It had surprised him when he first learned this. He always thought Adidas was an American shoe. He was also surprised to learn that the guy who founded the Puma shoe company was brother to the guy who founded Adidas. Impossible to believe, but true.

Moore's first athletic shoes as a boy had been Adidas. The three stripes meant that he might run faster than the other boys on the track team, even though he never would run faster. Nevertheless, Moore had kept faith with the logo ever since. He sat now at the airport gate in his Adidas blue nylon exercise clothes and it was funny he should be wearing this training outfit since he wasn't an exerciser —at least not since those early days on the track team.

Moore hated exercise—the monotony of it, the aches and pains that came with exercising; what's more, it was next to impossible to find a gym that he wanted to work out in. Moore thought hotel gyms were dirty, the equipment wasn't always safe, and they often had the same smells in them as the hotel cafeteria. Also, he didn't like sharing the cramped exercise rooms of hotels with other people of equally poor coordination and conditioning huffing and puffing and sweating and stinking. As a result, about the only exercise Moore got these days was running through airports to make connecting flights.

The worst situation of all was the powerless feeling Moore got while circling in a fixed flight pattern over an airport waiting to land, knowing that with each extended minute in the air the likelihood of meeting his connection dropped considerably. Then there was the landing, the waiting on the tarmac for a slot at an airport gate, and the impatient wait for people ahead of him to file off the airplane, then grabbing his overhead luggage and dodging through crowds in the retractable walkway and once out in the open he would start running, like O. J. Simpson in his glory years as a commercial huckster for Hertz.

There Moore was, countless times, running, lumbering more like it with little grace, his bag bouncing uncomfortably off his shoulder. Already he was out of breath and shuffling, hoping for a moving walkway—and there his gate was: number ten on the other side of the terminal, and the calls over the intercom: Last call for passengers on Flight 987. Last call!

Moore's shuffle turned into a trot, then reduced to a fast walk, then the pause to catch breath, then off to a trot again, and just as they were closing the doors he was within range to scream: Wait, hold the door, Flight 987 . . . and once he got on board the plane, there was the worry that his heart might burst from overexertion: his chest heaving, the sweat pouring off his temples, his pulse racing.

No, exercise wasn't for him, Moore thought, though he liked exercise suits. They were comfortable and they helped him get through security.

Moore hated security. It was a gift, his hatred and the endlessly changing rules of security, that terrorists had bequeathed to travelers like him. These Adidas exercise suits helped Moore deal with all the snags that invariably came with passing through.

Moore tried to dress and look as bland as possible. Secretly he worried that he might become bland. *It's fear*, Moore thought, *that keeps us honest in all this*. What was it Hamlet said, something of a bare bodkin in his famous speech? It was fear of the bodkin that kept you honest.

Moore sat and wondered a bit about that word. What did it mean? What was a bodkin? He knew it was a knife—but a metaphoric knife, perhaps, that kept one honest? For Moore, he supposed, his "bodkin," so to speak, was airport security. He was mildly intimidated by security. It was the part of travel, and by extension, of his job, that he least liked.

How many times had Moore awakened before dawn and lain in bed a few extra minutes in the privacy of his room, and he would say: Soon the day will begin and with it that great public ordeal of passing through airport security.

The two moments of his day couldn't be more radically opposed. The one, a moment of absolute privacy and quiet; the other a moment fraught with crowds, suspicion, worry, stress—and it all happened out in the open for everyone to see.

Moore had once or twice been pulled aside and patted down and had the wand waved over him. Both experiences were more humiliating and unpleasant than he had anticipated and they had left a mark on him. He had felt accosted, publicly singled out and eviscerated. *That's the wrong word*, he thought. He hadn't been "eviscerated," it was more like he had been mugged and there was nothing at all he could do about it while the folks who passed through the metal detectors unscathed observed him curiously trying to determine if he was indeed a malign threat.

There Moore stood, his arms up in the air. Law enforcement personnel—strangers with a badge—were putting their hands on his body. Who were they to touch him and no place was off-limits.

One guy had even touched his balls—it was repulsive and he almost followed an impulse to strike out at the guard, but he thought better of it. Next thing he knew the wand was being waved over him—but instead of a magic wand, it was a wand that sought out malevolent things: guns, explosives, knives, who knew what else? At a moment's notice, the wand could become a billy club meant to subdue him.

When Moore was pulled out of the crowd, he couldn't help wondering what it was about him that had drawn the suspicion of the security guards in the first place. Did he really look like someone who might blow up a plane? What does such a person really look like? He just wanted to get home as soon as possible. He wanted to pass through as invisibly as possible and yet they weren't letting him remain invisible. They were singling him out in a very public fashion.

Besides the debasement of being touched, it was humiliating. While their hands touched him Moore longed to go back to bed to that private moment beneath the sheets where he was alone, by himself, lost to the world.

There was no need to frisk Moore as a threat. He certainly didn't want to blow anyone up. He didn't love humanity per se. Airports turned him against people. Moore found he could strongly dislike someone because of some irritation that person caused him in the airport. However, in a pinch he could like anyone. Heck, he even liked his clients, many of whom weren't so easy to like. They were often small-minded, uninteresting, and protective of their margins. They were bland. Yet Moore could say he'd figured out a way to like all of his clients. It was part of his survival mechanism. *If I'm going to do this job, sales, I better figure out how to like the person I serve.*

And indeed he had. Moore sent his customers cards to commemorate their personal victories or holidays or birthdays. He was filled with remembrance. *How's Ricky doing?* He had asked one of his clients this very question yesterday morning. Ricky had leukemia and was only ten years old. It was a tragic story, yet he took the time to pay homage to Ricky's courage and to the courage of his customer.

No, Moore would never blow up a plane. He had better things to do. He might even prove a hero should he be called upon to take occasion against terrorists. Actually, Moore thought about it often. What if a terrorist should take over the plane? Moore girded himself for such eventualities. He referred to such occurrences as eventualities. *Should my plane eventually be taken over, I guarantee you I would do everything humanly possible to stop the terrorist's mission.* Moore had told friends and colleagues, not to mention folks who sat down next to him on the plane, that he wouldn't think twice about sacrificing himself to save the plane in the event of a terrorist attack. So why were they—why were these security guards pulling him aside to wave that wand over him?

Moore supposed afterward that it might have been related to the fact that he hadn't shaven and his beard, which was dark and grizzled, gave him a slightly dangerous or demonic look. Subsequently, Moore made sure always to shave before he went to the airport. Even if he had an afternoon flight, he would make sure to drop into some restroom or his hotel bathroom prior to flight and shave his beard off.

Moore hated shaving but he shaved often because he had such a heavy, quick-growing beard. The razor scraped his skin, which was so sensitive it pimpled under the blade. Despite his skin's sensitivity, he was aggressive with the blade because only multiple swipes seemed to get the hair follicles beneath the skin. He remembers all of a sudden Broadway Joe Namath with the glass knees. Broadway Joe and all those Noxzema skin-care commercials where he showed off his shaved legs. *Let Noxzema cream your face so the razor won't.* Moore hummed the jingle now as he sat there at the gate watching the snow fall on the tarmac.

47

Broadway Joe dropping back—in Super Bowl III, was it? Namath had predicted the Jets would win, hadn't he? It was in Miami. And there was Broadway Joe dodging around the pocket being hunted down by defensive linemen, and now pushed out of the pocket and at the last minute finding a man open in the end zone and hitting who in the end zone? Moore couldn't remember the receiver's name. Moore can almost see the ball flying in slow motion through the air, parting the arms of a defender and landing in the embrace of the receiver who pulls it close to his body, his toes hitting turf before he falls out of bounds. God, it was so beautiful when it was done right, he thought.

Moore wants to lean over in the chair and tell the guy sitting in the chair next to him, reading the paper, how football could be so beautiful and filled with grace it sometimes tore his heart out, the beauty. But the man next to him was absorbed reading the financials in the *Wall Street Journal*. Better to leave him alone than pester him with an inane observation about football.

As to doing anything malevolent on a plane, no. Not he. Moore had better things to do. Like get home and watch football in the privacy of his apartment, or better yet, wonder about that fleeting image he had just caught sight of moments ago: the image of the Woodsman who stakes out into the wilderness, saying goodbye to the disasters of his youth and proud to be a Woodsman at last: one with the land in a sacred unity.

There the Woodsman stands now on the Great Plains looking upward at the blue dome of a sky as yet unscarred by the white contrails of jets streaking overhead.

chapter 13
cumulonimbus calvus

Snow sifted down. It moved this way and that. For a while, Moore tried to track a single snowflake against the blur of other snowflakes in the storm. There's one—follow that one. There it is. No, there. No, that's it. Okay, that one there. Follow that one. It's slowly falling fluffily falling, wait now an updraft has it, now it's caught in a vicious downdraft. Wait—where did it go? I lost it in the tumult of the storm.

It was the duck and the rabbit phenomenon, Moore thought. He looked at the snow falling. Either you followed a single flake drifting this way and that, or you saw great volumes of snow flowing on currents of air, but it was impossible to follow both. It was either the duck: the single snowflake; or the rabbit: the great volume of snow being pushed on currents of air.

He also thought of Heisenberg and his great principle of uncertainty. Moore had first learned of this principle in college and he hadn't explored it beyond the class where the idea was first presented to him, but the idea that you could say either where a subatomic particle was or where it was going but you couldn't say both —that you could only see one side of reality: the duck, for instance, or the other side, the rabbit—thrilled him.

It thrilled him on two accounts: that you could know reality with incredible precision from one vantage point, but from another vantage point it was absolutely inscrutable. Moore loved that word, "inscrutable." In these times, Moore thought, what is needed is that which is inscrutable.

In a moment of time, harnessing a confluence of technologies, Google and other tech corporations too familiar to name had mapped, connected, and perceived the world with such completeness that the unknown world, the unexplored and hidden parts of it, seemed banished forever from our purview. The unknown no longer existed. With a touch on your device you could zoom to a rock pile on the side of Mt. Everest and see in fine detail the lichen growing on the rock and maybe even the footprint of a departed hiker.

Every part of the globe had seemingly been investigated; what had once seemed vast and unscalable—the Earth—was now described as a small, fragile ecosystem no longer containing lost unmapped places. It was bad enough, when, in the atomic age, it was thought that we could blow the place up—but even then it was a world with large swaths of unknown frontier. Now it was no longer so. From the vast deserts to the deep ocean trenches—not a jot of the Earth was left unexplored.

Scientists lived on both poles determining to a fine point how much longer the ice mantle would last in this ever-warming cocoon where conflagrations of fires raged, volcanoes erupted, ever-massive storms disabled human populations and released energy into the skies. But think of it: it was only one hundred years ago when the poles, against great adversity, had first been reached and now open water and arctic shipping lanes have replaced the thousands of miles of pack ice that polar explorers once marched across. It seemed too surreal to believe, that the ice was on the verge of a great melt and soon it would be a memory, and yet such was the case.

The once limitless equatorial forests that ringed the Earth were also being ruthlessly bulldozed under and torched only to be replaced and superseded by arid ranch land, or illicit drug crops, or sugar plantations, or lumberyard forest or surface mines that leveled the mountains or oil fields that besmirched the land, and on and on the depredations went faster by the day.

It was hard for Moore to read about all this stuff but he told himself that he must read about it. He took it as a solemn moral responsibility to keep up on how jungles were rapidly disappearing, the oceans befouled, the air black-stained by carbon toxins, and the ice caps liquidated.

As a result of the reduction of the Amazon rain forest, for instance, remote indigenous tribes were fast disappearing and even at this moment stories abounded in the newspapers and *National Geographic* magazine of one indigenous man in particular. He has been, for the past few decades, the last surviving member of his tribe and, aging without a spouse, he has no hope of recapitulating himself in a new generation. He lives alone in some remote region of the Amazon and scientists and ecotourists gather just out of range of the indigenous man monitoring his movements.

How does he seem to himself is the question . . . as alone in a vast untrammeled wilderness? Or does he realize that he inhabits a small protected patch of the Amazon that has been protected just for him and that all of his relatives have disappeared?

Moore read the story and tried to imagine himself as the last indigenous man of the Amazon wilderness, but in point of fact, it made Moore so unhappy and sad he stopped nearly as soon as he started. *We're just like that guy*, Moore thought: *the wilderness of our own unfoundedness is gone, and now we are exposed for all to see.*

In another instance, Moore read a valedictory story of a population of a few thousand lowland gorillas that had been discovered deep in the Rwandan rain forest. This discovery was greeted with relief: not just that there were a few more thousand gorillas than were previously thought to exist but that there could still be undiscovered populations of anything—and particularly of megafauna hidden in the forests whose hiddenness was still extant in this day and age.

Wildlife that had roamed the Earth had now been pushed to the margins and lived largely in protected national parks that were always under threat from poachers, farmers, and villagers, and those creatures that didn't make it into the parks were endlessly nearing the brink of extinction: they were hunted down to populations of single digits for their teeth or their tusks, for their horns or their hide. They were hunted to be stuffed like pillows and hauled back like tchotchkes to the hearth and home fire to fuel a conversation among guests of how the hunt had proceeded by guide and jeep and high-powered rifle and completed all before ten a.m. and then flown out by helicopter over Mt. Kilimanjaro.

The thought that evolution would continue to work on the remaining vestiges of wildlife on the planet to produce new species in the future seemed all but unlikely to Moore. Factory farms and mining both on land and at sea had put an end to notions of wilderness that existed only a generation ago. Now the oceans had been turned into factory farms where the last wild populations of fish were being harvested for sushi connoisseurs in deep landlocked urban centers. The wilderness and vast untrammeled diversity of fishes of the ocean exchanged for a plate of sushi to anyone in a mall who wanted to eat sushi on a Tuesday night! It all seemed unbelievable, but as Moore understood it, it was all too true.

Big Brother as Orwell imagined him would be wonderful, Moore thought; bring him back. Instead, we have a shrunken overpopulated planet. We have credit cards, GPS tracing systems, and the information trail that we leave like flotsam in the digital seas of the internet that keep track of our every move: all of these observance systems seemed more benign than Orwell imagined them, but what was truly frightening about them was that they were so successful and comprehensive in their observance that no dark unmapped space or action escaped their viewing. And should some strongman one day grab hold of this information, then what is benign—birthday wishes on social media and the connections of hundreds of unknown friends gabbing away without guile for all the world to see—might reduce us to enemies of the state. What we willingly put out there of ourselves in the digital universe was more human record than any previous autocrat in history could dream of having on us.

But more worrisome than that, it was as if technology itself were replacing the living.

And though it wasn't true yet, nevertheless it seemed that the great variety and amplitude of diverse living things was being tilled under, and a monoculture of humans and ants seemed likely the only species to exist in a few generations.

There were times Moore tried to imagine that the great intergenerational conversation between humans was broken by some calamity. He imagined the emergent generation without a linguistic connection or a historical road map to the remains that we left behind. Imagine some group of people with no connection—like that indigenous man, for instance, in the Amazon rain forest or some gnomic woodsman who only knew of the woods—imagine him or someone like him coming upon all of this then: the signs would be inscrutable, the machines and what purposes they were meant for would be impossible to divine, and the story of how it all came to be, of what it was all for and why? This story would be unknown and these questions would have no answer: they would be unfathomable and bottomless.

Moore imagined the universe tilting back to its own ignorance; it was the opposite pole from the direction we were headed and Moore wanted to go back that way a little bit. He wished for a little bit of that which was undiscovered, untrammeled, and unnamed; the unknowable and unquantifiable things that nevertheless bring value and comfort beyond words. The duck and the rabbit; himself versus the crowds.

He was at once a single, perishable, one-of-a-kind human with dark unknown dreams and thoughts of his own and yet he was a meaningless part of the blizzard; an endless iteration of the same human pattern and yet, at heart, he felt he was different—a new thing—and he felt this way if for no other reason than he had dreams that no one but he could experience; he had interior thoughts and emotions, feelings and sensations: a vast interior weather system of history and memory and connections that even he was only remotely conscious of but that was as vast as the weather system right there out-of-doors.

Sometimes it registered as an internal hum, sometimes as a howl, other times as a low unsung melody that made him unique in ways that were inexpressible and unknown to all.

I am me, Moore thought. I am Jim Moore. I travel and will continue to do so until I drop. I am unique. I am inscrutable. No one knows what I dream, or what he dreams, Moore thought, looking over at the man with the McDonald's meal. I'm every bit as unique and inscrutable as is that guy right across from me. That big guy right there across the gate stuffing his face with French fries.

chapter 14
cumulonimbus capillatus

Moore was born in Iowa—that's where most of his family was.
He wishes he could say he had a happy childhood. But it was neither
happy nor sad. It was merely bland. Whenever he thought of his
childhood he had a hard time picturing it. His dad . . . his mom . . .
the house; that he could picture. He could also picture the school
bus picking him up to take him to school, but that was about it.
Once or twice—in the heat of a romance—his lover had asked
him: *What was it like growing up on a small farm in Iowa?* Moore always
thought it a strange line of inquiry, this type of question.

What do you mean, what was it like growing up on a small farm in Iowa?
Same as growing up anywhere else, I suppose.

When this response solicited a frown, Moore had simply said, It
was fine.

No, seriously, he remembers one girlfriend saying, pressing him
for details, trying to get him to open up. What was it really like, Jim?
Give me details. Childhood on a small farm in Iowa . . .

Why do you ask?

I'm only trying to get you to open up.

I'm not a can or a clam that you can just pry open.

It's only a question, Jim. Just a bit of conversation. What was it really like growing up on a small farm in the Midwest? Can you tell me just one thing that you liked about it?

To humor her, Moore thought about it a moment. Here, let me close my eyes. He closed his eyes and he tried to fall through time down the ladder of memory, hoping to discover some unforgettable moment that he could share with his new girlfriend, but either he was disinclined to fall or there were no memorable moments because a second later Moore opened his eyes and said,

Just as I said. It was fine. Nothing to report. Nothing, as far as I can remember. It was all of a piece. It was a farm, what do you want me to say? That it was paradise on Earth? Because it wasn't!

The woman doing the inquiring was Rosemary. She was a tall woman with brown hair that curled at her shoulders. She wore turtle-neck sweaters in the winter that showed off her attractive figure and in the summer she wore these tantalizing sleeveless blouses—on one arm, just above the elbow, was a small tattoo of a heart and on the other arm was tattooed a tragic mask with a tear pouring out of the eye. Moore spent long hours staring at both of these tattoos—puzzling over them. What kind of a crazy person would tattoo these things on their body?—but never once did Moore ask her about them or what they meant.

Rosemary was so vivacious and filled with life that Moore was intimidated by her much of the time they were together. She chatted on endlessly about all sorts of things. She liked to tell the story over and over again how once, for instance, she had gotten drunk and, exiting the nightclub near two a.m., she had fallen down a huge flight of stairs and broken her back. She still managed to get to her feet, stumble to the curb, and hail a cab to drop her off at the emergency room. She told the story as an object lesson, though what the object of the lesson was, Moore was never able to determine: That

56

she was resilient beyond belief? That she was an occasional binge drinker? That she could live through this and laugh about it?

The X-rays confirmed what she suspected: a broken vertebra. She said she heard it snap. She beat the odds on recovery as well. Within four weeks she was on her feet again and going at the world full-tilt as if nothing had ever happened to her.

What was one supposed to do with a person who had that kind of grit, Moore thought. Had it been him, he'd still be lying on his back complaining of pain. Rosemary laughed about it too, and even though her back still gave her incredible pain, she didn't let it get between her and what she wanted to accomplish in life.

Her goal was nothing less than to become a federal judge one day and . . . and . . . and in her spare time she was writing a book, a memoir about her father!

Moore thought her a little bit crazy at times, and at times he even thought her a bit unhinged. On the other hand, he doesn't think he's ever known a smarter person. He often wondered why she shared all of this energy with him. He seemed plain by comparison. All of her talking gave him a complex. *I'm not nearly as smart as she is.* What's more, she was assertive when it came to sex and she used him, that's the way he later phrased it to a colleague of his; after he had disappointed her, she used him for her own sexual pleasure.

That doesn't sound all bad, said his colleague married fifteen years who was intrigued by the possibility.

It is bad, Moore pointed out, if you're the object—the tool of pleasure and all you want to do is come home and watch TV or go to bed exhausted and unmolested.

To which his colleague pointed out: You're foolish, Moore, foolish to complain. Foolish, foolish, foolish.

The fact is that Rosemary could talk about anything under the sun. She talked a blue streak, a red-hot streak, and a yellow streak all at once. She loved to chatter and she laughed compulsively at the funny, crazy, maddening things she had experienced in the day and during her life.

57

I often have nothing to say, can't think of a thing to say, and there she is describing her day as if it comprises a full lifetime. It doesn't seem real to me. I don't believe a person can experience so much.

Rosemary often liked to extemporize on her own childhood, which was filled with a seemingly endless number of characters she had known in her life, chief of whom was her father. She grew up in Chicago. Her father was a tavernkeeper. Moore had even visited her father's bar on Kimball and North Avenue in Humboldt Park. If he had been intimidated by Rosemary's energy he was downright frightened by the father. Her father had a sense of humor, of wit, of repartee that was deflating if you didn't know how to deal with it. Your father has a rapier wit, Moore later told her.

Oh?

The thing is.

Yes?

The thing.

No, go ahead. He liked you.

The thing is. No sooner do I meet him than he wants to slice and dice me. It was a hello, right? Not a jousting contest.

Rosemary distinctly frowned at this statement. This is one thing Moore could say for certain. He had disappointed Rosemary with that comment.

Moore doesn't remember exactly how he and Rosemary had hooked up. It was probably at a party, but one day he saw her at a coffee shop, and they exchanged hellos as if they had known each other forever. He sat down to chat with her and before he knew it they were in the middle of a full-blown romance.

The whole romance lasted two and a half years, which was the longest time Moore had ever been with anyone. Prior to Rosemary, Moore seldom had a romance that extended beyond the six-month period. He doesn't know why this was exactly, though it was often the case that the woman would find herself less and less intrigued with Moore and before six months were up she had left for a different man.

It was all the same to Moore. As far as he could tell, he had never been in love. He didn't understand the sort of obsessive love that brought couples together, sometimes with disastrous results. There was one couple he knew—they were so obsessed with each other that they had gone after each other with all sorts of weapons: bottles, knives—it was hand-to-hand combat. The abuse was shocking. Moore had heard them screaming in the middle of the night at each other. Their voices came through the walls and he wondered what held them together. Surely, no relationship can sustain this for long, he thought. And yet there they were in daylight hours so in love with each other they were inseparable—she had a black eye, he had his arm in a sling. How can you live like that? Moore wondered. And yet here was evidence of it: obsessive love that was greater than the hate and anger that threatened to split it apart.

Better to leave off quietly in the night, Moore thought, the way he always seemed to leave, or worse, waking in the morning to discover she had gone. No explanation. So long. See you later. It was nice while it lasted. But where was the. Where was the. Oh, you know. The. The passion. Where was it, honey? It was nowhere to be found. I'd rather you took swipes at me. Instead, you fell asleep in the chair while I told you of my day. Shame on you!

Moore sat there in his chair at the airport thinking about it. What was there to think about? Why was there any thought whatsoever about this sort of thing? Hell, he was in an airport. He was waiting for an airplane that wouldn't fly until the snowstorm dissipated. He was suffering from a lack of oxygen. His back and legs hurt from sitting too long. He was tired of staring at humanity. Wasn't that enough? Why was he forced to think about things like this on top of it? *Give me a break,* he thought. *Internal hum! More an internal racket. Leave me alone.*

Moore waved his hand as if swatting something away and went back to watching at the gate and there in front of him appeared two noisy boys chasing each other with Matchbox cars. The snow fell on the tarmac. There was no end in sight.

chapter 15
cumulonimbus incus

The heavy man opposite Moore at the gate packed up his McDonald's and walked over to the garbage can. He disposed of the cardboard and paper packaging, along with the cup, the lid, the straw, the ketchup and mustard packets that he had torn open with his teeth and squirted into the lid of his Big Mac container like tubes of toothpaste. Where was this guy from? Moore wondered. Where was he going? Where were any of us going?

Then there was the annoying woman jabbering on the phone right across from him at the gate. Moore had to admit, the woman was not unlovely. She was intensely attractive. Perhaps it was her attractiveness that annoyed Moore, or rather he allowed himself to become annoyed by her as a way to fend off the power of her beauty. She kept talking and talking. It was relentless how much she could talk on her phone but what was it she was actually saying?

She was clearly the mother of the young boys maybe three and five years old who were running around with the Matchbox Hot Wheels cars. He concluded that they were partly to blame for his feeling of claustrophobia. The mom sat surrounded by luggage, her legs kicked up on one of the bags. She wore a simple red T-shirt and blue jeans. Everyone else was swaddled with winter clothes. She seemed to care less about the weather conditions. She had her hair up: it was a gorgon of curls. Moore thought it astonishing, particularly as the lobes of her ears and her long neck were revealed. The long neck muscles and tendons strained beneath her skin like carved soap, he thought all of a sudden, her head tilted toward the phone that she held intimately to her ear. And her skin probably smells as nice as soap too. She was lovely no doubt, but would she please stop chattering.

The kids ran up and down the aisles banging on the glass windows, playing tag, screeching—they were playing keep-away: one kid stole the car from the other and around and around they ran, stumbling into his bag, knocking it over. Moore repositioned his bag, took his coffee cup and moved it off a small table into the holder on his arm rest. A moment passed and running through the aisle again, the boys knocked his bag over again. He looked over at the mom but she didn't take any notice. She was jabbering away into her phone, having, as far as Moore could surmise, an absolutely inane conversation with her sister about which presents should be returned to the store—

Yes yes yes no uh-hunh uh-hunh sure I dunno go ahead why not ha ha ha ha that's what Harry says yes oh my God you're kidding me no you're joking please okay so yes yes no but—

On she droned. Moore supposed it passed for conversation, but what type of conversation? Was there any content exchanged? Any information? The woman spoke in confidential tones. She absent-mindedly searched the ends of her long black hair for splits and when she found one she gave the hair follicle a gentle tug, letting it drift up slightly pulled by a small current of air, and then down it fell to the airport's terrazzo floor.

The flotsam and detritus of an ever-decaying humanity, Moore thought, with a touch of disgust—that's what these large-public-airport spaces ultimately are: the repository of what's lost while waiting for planes that don't go: flaked skin, dried mucus, exhaled CO_2 from still-living bodies, the release of other gases, mites, dandruff, hair, fingernail clippings, lice, germs, sweat, bacteria, blood, bedbugs, remnant fecal matter, urine, semen, viruses, endless amounts of lint, and God knows what else as we make our slow descent back to cosmic matter.

What volume of this stuff, exhalation, expectoration, sternutation, perspiration, salivation, ejaculation, menstruation, parturition, lactation, exfoliation, epilation, lacrimation, eructation, flatulation, regurgitation, urination, defecation, secretion, spontaneous exsanguination, and suppuration was shed unto the floors at the gates of airports like this all over the world? And the trouble crews must have keeping places like this clean.

Moore saw the janitor staff—they blended in with the crowds pushing dust brooms on the shiny terrazzo floors. Automatic mopping machines sucked up spills and it all sloshed around in the primordial soup of the machine's detergent. Where does all of this effluvia go? Down the drain, through the rivers, and discharged out to the seas whence it all came.

On the woman talked, twisting her gorgon curls while her kids scooted between travel bags dodging this way and that banging into things, screaming, laughing, falling, crying. Up on their feet, then down again, then moving along shimmying shammying this way and that. Moore looked over to the man next to him who was reading the *Wall Street Journal*. The man seemed not to have noticed the boys. He was oblivious, locked in his own world of thought. The woman on the phone, beautiful though she was, didn't seem to notice either. She had her own pressing concerns gossiping with some other soul at the other end of the wireless signal. Cell phone towers were punched into the landscape from one end of the country to the other broadcasting what? An enormous cacophony of blab. Towers and towers of blab. It was a heap and a dunghill of droning noise.

Why can't that mom just get off her damn phone and control her kids? That's the way with parents these days. They're self-absorbed by all this electronic gadgetry. It takes them away from the more fundamental task of tending to their children. Moore thought back to the phrase *It takes a village* and thought—*Yes it does, with parents like this woman who lets her kids run wild, strangers can't help but get involved.*

The gentleman sitting off to Moore's right looked over his reading glasses at Moore, and then he looked disapprovingly at the woman then back at Moore. In a comradely moment he nodded and seemed to imply that these children were seriously out of control—and with a mom like that, no wonder!

A moment later one of the boys—the older of the two—leaped onto the man's lap, screaming: Daddy, Benjy is going to Chicago with his mom. He's going just like us, on the plane.

The gentleman looked over at the woman and smiled at her. She lifted her eyes a moment and smiled back. Then he gave the boy a hug and set him on the ground, where the boy took off running after his little friend, Benjy. Was the gentleman also attracted to the woman? Hard to say, though the exchanged smile made Moore feel a bit left out. Without having mutual kids in common, so much of society is shut off from him. It was a shame.

Moore looked closely at the woman, trying to get her attention just as the gentleman had, but either she didn't see him or she sensed he was angry and chose to ignore him. *Am I angry at her or do I want her to acknowledge me?*

Moore imagined what she must be like. Hollow, he thought. Beautiful but hollow and empty. But those eyes. They were anything but empty. They were filled with restless energy, with searching inquisitiveness, with longing and disappointment. They were eyes not unlike his, he thought. He was no different than any of them. *Let's face it, he thought. You sit here in judgment but you are hardly different. You're no better. After all, you consume the same products they consume.*

You listen to the same music. You read the same news and know many of the stories of the same celebrities. Actress X is having a nervous breakdown, that much Moore knew. She was the latest in an endless procession of stars to be having a nervous breakdown at the end of their formative career with the knowledge that what lies beyond is merely the void of the rest of their lives and the endless diminishment of their vast resources—spent mindlessly on stuff. Moore knew the stories of weight loss and loss; was just as titillated by Star M's fluctuations in weight as he was by the death of Actor Y: a good actor meeting a tragic end. But once ended, what does Actor Y know or care? Nothing—though his legend grows perhaps faster on account of his untimely death.

No, Moore wasn't any different than any of the folks surrounding him. He was as culturally situated and as much a product of the times as were they. He had his apartment, which was furnished with many of the same items as everyone else who shops at Target and Walmart. He had blue bath mats, nice pull-down shades, a Ralph Lauren comforter with 1,200-thread-count Egyptian cotton. He collected cuff links that he purchased at Men's Warehouse. He owned a set of martini glasses that he had purchased at Crate & Barrel. He wore shoes with Vibram lug soles from L.L.Bean and a polyester jacket from North Face. He drove a Toyota SUV that he kept parked on the street outside his apartment. He collected guns: he owned a Remington .350 magnum with a Capo sight, and a Browning double-barrel twelve-gauge shotgun that he purchased at Walmart. He too had an Apple laptop, a smartphone filled with the latest apps. He loved to shuffle between his entertainment apps, his news apps, and his work-related apps. He compulsively checked his email and followed the torrent of commentary on social media. He often envied others their newer, more beautiful technology. *If I could only afford it,* Moore thought. *I would be the first person in line to buy new technology as it was created.* Yet here he was, cursing those who were absorbed using their handhelds!

I don't go to church and maybe she does and maybe that's how we're different. But still I'm not brainwashed by all of this consumerism. I haven't been zombified by all of this buying. My coffee is personal to me even though I bought it at Starbucks and while I drink it I let my mind go in whatever direction it wants to go. Oh, don't ask me what I'm thinking, Moore thought in reference to Rosemary; she was always asking him: Tell me what you're thinking.

I'm not thinking about anything.

Oh, sure you are, she pressed. Your mind is somewhere else I can tell.

No, it isn't.

Yes it is.

No.

Yes.

No.

Listen. If your mind were here you would have followed what I've been telling you for the last fifteen minutes but I can tell you're not here. You smile and nod your head, Jim, but you're not paying any attention.

My mind is here.

Let Noxzema cream your face so the razor won't.

No, it's not here, Rosemary said.

He looked over at the board and saw that no time was yet posted for his departure. There wasn't even anyone at the check-in counter of his gate.

I was telling you something important . . .

The Woodsman was crossing a stream. *This is a very important part right here*, Moore thought. The logs had fallen across the stream and though they were huge they were rotten and large slabs of moss had collected on the bark. The greenery of the deep forest was blinding. The forest smells were terrific. One false move and you can slip off this log into the fast-moving stream below. Moore looked up at the overhanging branches and considered if any of those branches were strong enough to get him across the stream. *Why do I want* to get across this stream anyway? Oh yes, because of the way the land opens up on the other side of the stream while it becomes impass-able on this side. Moore wanted to ask the Woodsman if he had ever returned to that prostitute at The Lawg Caybun but thought better of it.

I took a bit of codeine today and I've been out of it. Hello, are you listening to me?

There is nothing to report, he remembers telling Rosemary. There is nothing to report of growing up in farm country.

Oh please. There must be. I grew up on a city block in the middle of a thousand clapboard houses and apartment buildings. I have an infinite number of things to report.

Then report away . . .

But I've already told you everything. It's your turn to share.

Rosemary smiled at him.

There's nothing to share, he said.

You're kidding me, she said.

Land of sky-blue wa-aters.

No I'm not kidding you. Why would I kid about something so stupid?

That isn't stupid.

Yes it is.

No it isn't.

Yes.

No.

Was I in love? Moore wondered.

He stared at the woman on the phone. She paused her torrent of words and lifted her eyes to his. She smiled quietly at him. Moore smiled back, confused. At this she dropped her eyes back to her split ends and resumed her talking.

chapter 16
cumulonimbus mammatus

As a boy growing up in Iowa, Moore used to go hunting with his father. He loved hunting pheasants and rabbits. He had a Stevens pump sixteen-gauge shotgun that his father had given him. Where was that shotgun now? In the rafters or crawl space of his parents' home, no doubt, though there was no claiming it: he had long ago sold the place after his parents had died.

Moore would like to have that shotgun now if only to stir the memory of those cool autumn mornings moving through the cornfields with his father. Yes, those were the days!

Moore remembers driving with his dad to the hunting site in the twilight of early morning. He attempted to be stoic in preparation for the hunt, but he wasn't by nature a stoic kid. His stoicism or what passed for stoicism would come later—from years of grinding work in adulthood.

As a kid he felt his heart constrict in anticipation, but anticipation of what? In anticipation of *being*, Moore thought. *I was anticipating being alive and those moments in the car ride to the hunt*—it was anticipation that was the joy and life of the thing. He sees this quite clearly now, though he didn't see it at the time.

Before they began hunting, his father would pour a cup of coffee from a thermos, and from a silver screw-top flask he'd spill a bit of whiskey into the drink. They'd lean up against the car—a 1964 white Ford Fairlane with the round red taillights. Moore remembers sitting on the red vinyl upholstery. He also remembers driving in it one day with his father coming home from the store when the engine blew up on them and he was startled when his father cursed the car: Piece of shit, this Ford! his father yelled in exasperation. It was the only time his dad had sworn and it made a more lasting impression on Moore than the car engine that had just exploded and caught fire.

That day out hunting for pheasants, his dad was leaning up against the car, making small talk about the weather or the clouds— his father loved to talk about and analyze the cloud formations rolling in from the horizon like white text on a blue scroll or buses and whales larger than skyscrapers, depending. Of course there was the occasional colossal vortex cloud that reminded one of the things done in Hiroshima and Nagasaki. There were also clouds that reminded Moore of Dairy Queen ice cream cones, and even now, as he thought about it, he felt a longing in his heart to be back at a small-town Dairy Queen, on a hot summer day, sticking his tongue into some cold soft-serve ice cream. He also liked those anvil cloud formations just before a storm that hung off the base of a supercell and looked like massive plows rolling in to cleave the prairie with strokes of lightning.

All the clouds had perfect names and his father liked to iterate them as if they were mantras put up to stave off an all-too-soon self-extinction, for it was all too soon that his father did indeed self-extinct: only a few years later when Moore was in high school. Moore had been sitting in math class when his mom appeared startlingly in the doorway of his classroom and broke uncontrollably, compulsively into a face of excruciating angles and tears and Moore sat there not knowing what to do: whether to run toward her or away from her and so he just sat there paralyzed in his seat until his teacher quietly said his name: Jim, collect your books, please. You may be excused from class.

After it was all over—his father had blown the back of his head off with a twelve-gauge shotgun—after the burial, Moore felt embarrassed to be in that class for the rest of the year, and even now he feels the shame of it. The whole useless goddamned pitiful shame of it.

His dad had been passionate about clouds. He had been a member of the Iowa Cloud Appreciation Society and he knew every cloud beneath the sun. His dad repeated the cloud names while leaning against the car with his coffee and whiskey and Moore learned them too first by listening to his dad chant them and then later from a memorandum that Moore had found among his father's papers: a memorandum from the Iowa Cloud Appreciation Society that Moore later memorized. It listed many of the more common species and varieties of cloud to blow in on the atmosphere in various weather systems and even now Moore liked to repeat their names as if they were his own private kaddish chanted to express gratitude for his father's life, his father's love of the clouds, and to dispel the unending disquiet and confusion that his dad's death by self-inflicted gunshot wound had bequeathed to him. It had become his song of praise. It also had become a way to numb himself from the pain.

cumulus fractus, cumulus humilis, cumulus mediocris, cumulus congestus; stratocumulus castellanus, stratocumulus lenticularis, stratocumulus stratiformis; stratus fractus, stratus nebulosus, stratus opacus, stratus translucidus, stratus undulatus; cumulonimbus calvus, cumulonimbus capillatus, cumulonimbus incus, cumulonimbus mammatus, cumulonimbus pannus, cumulonimbus pileus, cumulonimbus praecipitatio, cumulonimbus spissatus, cumulonimbus velum, cumulonimbus tuba, cumulonimbus virga; altocumulus

70

perlucidus; altostratus duplicatus; mammatus; altostratus nebulosus, altostratus opacus, altostratus pannus, altostratus praecipitatio,
altostratus radiatus, altostratus translucidus, altostratus undulatus,
altostratus virga; cirrostratus nebulosus; nimbostratus pannus, nimbostratus praecipitatio; cirrus castellanus; nimbostratus virga

It was a pile of cloud names piled high like a cloud; piled like a
cumulonimbus pileus, a cloud formation that indicates a storm has
passed. His father talked of the clouds as if they might have some
providential impact on the course of their day. His father tracked
barometric pressures, the rise and fall of which directly influenced
the movement of small game. His dad explained that barometric
pressure affects the clouds, and the behavior of small game was tied
to the cloud cover.

Moore had loved his father for all of his wisdom and for his love
of weather and clouds, and he wished that his father, like that old
Stevens single pump-action sixteen-gauge, could be reclaimed, but
alas they were both gone, and now Moore felt so alone.

Moore's dad talked and as he talked he looked off at the trees and
wondered aloud if they would bag any animals today. What do you
think, Jim? What does the barometric pressure seem like to you? Can
you judge it from the clouds?

Moore would take a look at the clouds and try to guess the cloud
names, and, by the likes of them, whether the barometric pressure
was up or down. Moore came to understand that a rapid downward shift in pressure meant that the animals would be out of their
hutches searching for food, while a low barometric pressure and foul
conditions meant it might be better to stay home and hunker down
because that's likely what the animals were doing. Blue skies or light
cloud cover, on the other hand, was always a good day to hunt.

In the morning chill their dog, Lady, a Brittany spaniel, would already be off and running through the mowed-down cornstalks in search of animal smells. Look at her go, Jim! his dad would say.

Around the perimeter of the farm field, which sloped gently toward a creek, was a large stand of trees and up and along the creek was a small forest of oak and maple still with some brown and red autumn leaves clinging to the branches. It was an old wood grove that had very little undergrowth. The farmer kept a few salt blocks in the woods and a tree stand for deer, but they wouldn't be going into the woods today because they were hunting pheasants and rabbits. They liked to work the perimeter of the woods, and farther along were some railroad tracks with a bit of untilled wilderness on either side of the rails. They liked to walk along the tracks and see if Lady could scare up any pheasants or rabbits.

While they stood in the morning chill, Moore saw that the earth was turned over. It was black and clotted with cornstalks roughly poking out. When you stepped on this kind of soil you sank a bit unless the ground was frozen, and then you walked carefully in the trenches the tiller had made. His dad sipped his coffee; poured himself another cup and spilled whiskey into it from the flask. Moore made sure his hunting vest had enough shotgun shells and that his silver hand warmer in a red felt bag was working.

Moore liked his hand warmer. He had received it earlier in December as a pre-Christmas gift. He liked the smell of the low-burning butane fuel, and the warmness that the device provided. He remembers long days hunting and it wouldn't be until three in the afternoon after being out in the cold all day when he'd notice his hand warmer cooling down. At that point they were usually done with their hunt anyway, and packing the trunk of the car with any birds or rabbits they shot. In college, Moore purchased a Zippo lighter that had the same shape as the hand warmer and the same smell when you lit it. At that point in his life, the hand warmer was already a memory that the Zippo at the flicking of the sparking wheel would instantly conjure and there Moore would be again, out in the field with his dad, hunting, Lady fanned out in front, her tail wagging, her nose to the ground zigzagging through the brush in pursuit of mysterious animal scents.

Oh, how about that time, Moore thought, when Lady was killed. It stopped his heart even now to think on it. It may have even been that morning. His father put the flask back in his pocket, and the thermos back in the car. He closed the doors without locking them. Together, Moore and his dad walked parallel to each other through the tilled-over field. Moore tried to be hyperalert. In his youth growing up in Iowa he used to dream of hunting. It was the thing he most loved to do, but as an adult with all of this travel and the pressing responsibility of having to be one of the main income earners for his company, Moore felt he had lost some vital interest in hunting. The human population had grown so much since he was a kid, the animals pushed into ever smaller quarters of wilderness, that he felt more than ever it was unfair to try to snuff out what few animals had managed to survive this late into human history.

Nevertheless, Moore was dreaming of it now: he and his dad were walking in a field. Lady scared up a rabbit in front of his father. His dad shot twice, *bang-bang*, and the rabbit kept zigzagging, bounding, trying to find shelter. Moore took a shot—*pow*—and he saw where the pellets hit three feet behind the rabbit, kicking up a bit of dust, and the rabbit was gone. They continued to work the field and was that a red fox he spotted by the railroad track? His father wasn't certain but let's go check it out. They worked their way over to the railroad track and sent Lady into a bit of brush alongside the rails.

Suddenly a fox did scare up and went bounding down the center of the railroad tracks and Lady gave chase running after the fox. The fox and dog were three quarters of a mile down the track when a train emerged from under a viaduct. The fox jumped off the tracks but Lady froze, staring at the headlight of the train. Moore remembers that he and his dad screamed at Lady to scare her off the tracks. His dad reached for his flask and hurled it at the dog, but his throw was wide of the mark and fell short. The train conductor gave a few tugs at the horn, and in a moment it was over. Lady had been run over by the train. It was the most heartbreaking thing Moore had ever experienced up until that time. It was his dog, he had loved Lady, and there she was crumpled up, cut in two on the tracks. It didn't seem possible. One moment she was here. The next minute torn apart: an unrecognizable carcass of her formerly buoyant, playful self.

Moore promised himself he wouldn't cry, but he thought he would burst. They walked back to the car where his dad had a spade and they dug a shallow hole in the frozen ground, each taking turns, right next to where she had been run over. Moore said a prayer as he laid her in the grave but he felt like a fool. Who prays over a dog? It seemed sacrilegious to say the least. His dad was as good as could be through the whole catastrophe. Looks like she didn't know what was coming, Jim. Those were his father's exact words. He placed his hand on his son's shoulder and then said: Let's get out of this cold and go home.

Moore remembers the long drive home. The heater of the car burned up his feet as he drifted off to sleep to find what he so often looked for when the perimeter of his heart was hurt with pain. He closed his eyes and there in the distance he could just make him out . . . the Woodsman.

chapter 17
cumulonimbus pannus

Where the hell did he go, Moore wondered. Moore was breathing hard for oxygen and there in a clearing he saw the Woodsman sitting on a log waiting for him.

Have you been following me? the Woodsman asked.

Yes.

Why do you come back to the past to bother me, Jim? There must be something better than trying to track me down.

Moore looked eye-to-eye at the Woodsman and attempted to answer as honestly as possible: I suppose I want to know what your life is like.

My life? The Woodsman let out a loud explosive laugh. I hope you didn't kill yourself trying to find me to discover what my life is like.

I did.

Well, I hate to tell you, partner, but my life ain't worth getting interested in. It's more work than I care for, but I go along with it. I always say: If it don't kill me it'll make me stronger, and the rate I'm going I'll be the strongest guy in the world before long. Either that or a dead man, I suppose. Either way, there won't be a person in the world who cares because it's a lonesome existence. If it weren't for this whore I know and see every year around Christmastime in the winter or the Fourth of July in the summer, I don't know how I'd get along. But I get along in my way. I try not to bother anyone. Here, let me show you something.

Me? Moore asked. You want to show me something?

You didn't travel all this way in your mind for nothing, I don't suppose, the Woodsman said. Okay. This is what I want to show you, but you have to follow me deep into the woods. Do you think you can do that?

Yes, of course.

With those funny shoes you got on, I don't know . . .

I'll do my best. What else do I have to do? I'm just stuck in an airport waiting and I'm tired of waiting with nothing to do.

Okay, then do this. Follow me. Be careful and watch your step. All sorts of hidden traps and snares and things that'll take you down in a wild woods like this. But don't you worry too much. I've taken a bit of the woods down myself. So many years cutting on the long saw and chopping. Watching the old trees fall down. I suppose the woods has a right to figure its own way out to chop you and me down with a snare once in a while.

The Woodsman looked Jim over and shook his head. Is this what they dress in nowadays? What do you call this?

This is an Adidas exercise suit, Jim said. This jacket is called a zippy.

This red-and-black-checked wool jacket does fine by me, I suppose, the Woodsman said. I'll be surprised if that zippy holds up. I'll try to keep it steady but easy so you don't fall too far behind again.

Moore followed the Woodsman best he could. It was hard going through the woods and brush. He overleaped countless streams and scuttled over moss-covered granite boulders, one of which caused him to slip but not fall for he was able to reach onto an overhanging branch, which thankfully didn't snap. Instead, the branch had a bit of spring in it, and with the help of the spring Moore was able to leap over the stream.

76

The stream wended its way down from up above, moving through the forest. It rushed down in spots with alarming force and the noise of it echoed up into the high tops of the trees. The air was filled with the water's mist. Birds were chirping and singing; it sounded like a festival. At other spots there would be deep clear pools of water, and the sound of the birds reflecting off the still water made them seem closer at hand.

Moore kept running through the woods, sometimes going uphill, sometimes down, there was no pathway, it was enough to keep an eye out for the red of the always disappearing Woodsman who sauntered with great ease through the thickets of brambles, up and over fallen logs, and splashing across shallow streams.

Hey there, the Woodsman howled, hiyya!

And off Moore went running. His zippy got snagged in a patch of briars and thorns, his pant leg was torn on a jutting juniper branch, but all in all his clothes and he were holding up if not quite as easily as the Woodsman; still, he was doing better than he thought possible and always there was the stream coming back into view. The stream had emerged and disappeared so many times that now Moore was apprehending that they were following the waterway with its splashing falls and shallows and deep pools.

In one part of the woods the giant hemlock trees spired to an awesome height and the boughs were up there in the blue distance; the virgin hemlock trees rose from a forest that had stood unscathed for how many eons? *What is an eon*, Moore wondered, as he stood there looking up at the sky that seemed pierced by the jagged tip of a giant fir and then it occurred to him: an eon is a moment of time as grand as an ancient tree. Maybe longer.

The woods were shadow; patches of meadow and dappled light came into view. For a moment there was a solemn stillness and what is this? It appeared apparition-like, standing right there in front of him. Was it some kind of deer with those antlers or was it an elk or something grander? Whatever it was, it was the hugest antlered

77

animal Moore had ever seen and the animal lent majesty to the sacred space. Moore paused to watch the animal move, bowing its head slightly so the antlers showed forth, and then it tilted its neck as if it too were suggestively motioning for Moore to come along and so Moore was off running again, now following the Woodsman, now following the antlered animal.

Moore ran sidelong for some time along some limestone bluffs with deep grooves worn into the side by wind and time and in some parts there were caves hollowed out of the rock. He carefully followed narrow pathways on cliffs that were overhung with limestone ledges where he could see the stratification of geologic time, and at a bend on the narrow pathway there was a clearing and he saw out over the countryside, which, out beyond these woods, was ravaged by logging, picked clean and cleared, stumped and stubbled with the remains of a fallen forest. And there, out in the distance, was that white-topped mountain.

Hiyya, he heard up ahead, and off Moore went running back into the woods and climbing. The river came into view again, burbling up from some subterranean rocky place surrounded by large primitive ferns whose fronds unfurled in the mist. Moore ran dancing and jumping and crisscrossing the stream. The large antlered animal running up ahead seemed to be doing the same, and farther up ahead the ever-disappearing red coat of the Woodsman in those tall leather boots with all those eyelets sauntering, a picture of strength and primal vitality.

Who knows how long Moore had been going following the antlered animal and the Woodsman or how much farther there was to run. After a moment, Moore paused again to gather his strength by another pool in the river: the chittering of birds was close at hand. He caught his breath and stood looking into the deep pool at his own reflection and he wondered what he was looking at. *Is this a reflection of me I'm looking at or is it the remembered reflection of myself staring back at me in a remembered pool of water in a wood that I imagine as I sit waiting for an airplane?* But what remembered pool? Moore couldn't remember any such pools from any past moment of his actual life.

Nevertheless, the pool glimmered now before him. Down beneath the surface of the water were tiny little minnow trout darting about in the clear and rippled translucence of the flowing water, and beneath them there was gravel and sand and a log poking out of the gravel bed. He saw the reflection in the pool of water of the ruddy-faced Woodsman staring back at him.

Hiyya, are you coming? the Woodsman said, crooking his finger, encouraging Moore to come along.

Give me a minute, Moore said, I'm catching my breath.

The Woodsman leaped from a couple of boulders and appeared by his side.

Look down in that pool of water, the Woodsman said. What do you see?

I don't know what I see. Am I looking at a pool of water or am I staring into a remembered pool of water at my reflection, which looks like some other version of myself staring back at me?

I know what you mean, the Woodsman said.

Oh yeah? How so?

Because, the Woodsman said, sometimes at night if I'm lying beneath the open sky and stars are out in abundance, I'll drift off and I won't know in my own imagination where I am. Whether I'm here in these woods or someplace far off. Don't you think that's unusual? To dream of things we've never seen before: things we don't even understand?

Freud would probably say it was impossible.

Who are you talking about, this Freud? the Woodsman asked.

He's after your time, I suppose, Moore said.

It's something else to have you here, the Woodsman said with a smile, in your funny shoes wearing that . . . what do you call that thing you're wearing?

79

An Adidas zippy.

Yes, an Adidas zippy . . . The Woodsman emphasized "zippy" like a child.

Do you mind if I try it on? the Woodsman asked.

No, go ahead, Moore said. Perhaps you'll let me try on your lumberman's jacket as well.

Oh sure. Go ahead.

The Woodsman took off his black-and-red jacket and handed it over while Moore divested himself of his Adidas zippy. The Woodsman tried on the polyester zippy, pulled at the lapels and watched it stretch.

This is something else, the Woodsman said. He zipped it up and down and reached into the pockets. He pulled out Moore's keys and looked at them. In the other pocket were Moore's wallet, his phone, and some change. Is this what our money has become? the Woodsman asked, holding the coins in his hand. Let me see if I can guess what this is: a quarter?

Yes.

And whose face is this on the front?

George Washington.

The president?

Yes.

And what's this?

A dime. It's worth ten cents.

Who's on the face of this one?

John F. Kennedy.

Who was he?

He was a president that served in the early sixties, that is the 1960s. Under his leadership America became the first country to send a man to the moon.

A man to the moon? You tell me that's possible! Now I know I'm dreaming.

And would you believe even now we have spaceships flying to the stars?

80

Why, I'll be!

That other thing there. Do you know what that is?

The Woodsman looked carefully at the phone, turning it over, trying to figure out what this puzzling object was.

I have no idea. I have never seen such a thing.

That, my friend, is a cell phone. They call it a smartphone. I can talk to anyone in the world instantly with that thing. What's more, it ties into the internet, and from that an alarming bit of the world's information is available to me with the touch of the glass screen.

The internet?

It's almost like one of those fabled crystal balls, but even more magical. I'm sorry for even mentioning it, Moore said. Here I was thinking you lived the good life and now I've gone and spoiled it by telling you of all of our modern technology. Is it making us any smarter is the question. In the end, I think it only hurts. But that is a different story.

I wouldn't even know how to work this thing.

I don't suppose you would, nor would I recommend trying to figure it out. Leave it to your posterity to suffer.

Moore tried on the Woodsman's jacket. It fit loosely. It was a weighty wool jacket that smelled of pine resin and sweat. He pulled the collar up against his neck, and the sweat of the collar reminded him of his own sweat. It was worn at the wrists and the entryway to the pockets. He put his hands in the pockets and deep in the pockets he felt lint and a few pine needles.

Not much in the way of money in your own jacket.

No. I'm broke, the Woodsman said. I've been broke my whole life. Never had money for long. I work to survive, and each day I work I get another day of survival. Not much more than that. See, I told you it wasn't much of a life . . .

But I like this jacket, Moore said. Moore ran his palms across the coarse wool.

Maybe one day, the Woodsman said, if I take a shine to you, I'll let you have it. Can I look in your wallet? See what you have in it?

Sure.

The Woodsman opened Moore's wallet. He counted up the bills. There were three hundred and twenty-seven dollars. He laid the items from the wallet out on the giant stump of a fallen tree. Moore looked around him. Nature was so wild and untrammeled except for this stump. It was the widest stump he had ever seen.

The Woodsman whistled through his teeth. My oh my! That's more money than I've made my whole life's labor chopping trees.

I like to carry cash when I travel, Moore said. In case of emergencies.

Where do you travel?

I fly, crisscrossing the continent in commercial jet aircraft. It's not as glamorous as it seems. The air on board the planes tends to be bad, it makes for hard breathing especially for someone with asthma.

There's that word again.

The planes are crowded. They pack you into these things cheek-and-jowl like sardines in a can. Of course, in business class or first class they give you a little extra room, but my company, such as it is, prefers that I do all this travel coach. It's my penance, I suppose.

The Woodsman thumbed through the credit cards and insurance cards; the driver's license and worker ID card, and in one compartment of the wallet was crammed a dozen or so business cards.

Moore continued: You get jammed in next to these people on the planes, often there's not enough room, and you just sit there suffering waiting for the flight to be over. An awful lot of time is wasted on the tarmac waiting for the plane to take off or waiting for a gate where the plane can park. I can't tell you how many countless hours of my life I have spent either in the air or waiting to get into the air. And of course, there are the airports. Many of them are fine places architecturally, but to be honest—with security, and the crowds, and everything else I wouldn't care if I never stepped into another airport as long as I live. Matter of fact, I'm stranded in an airport right now because of weather.

82

What are all these cards? the Woodsman asked, flipping through Moore's wallet.

The plastic card you have in your hand is a credit card. It's now a form of money. That other card there is a bank card. I can slide that card into a machine and pull cash directly out of my account. Those cards there are the names of my associates at other businesses that I work with. I usually empty my wallet of business cards between trips, so those dozen or so cards are all the new contacts I made on this particular business trip. I type them into my computer.

A computer? the Woodsman asked.

Again, please, let's just assume there are things we each know that the other won't. No need to explain everything.

The Woodsman looked in all the pockets of Moore's wallet, and in one interior pocket pushed in beneath the fold was the black-and-white photograph of a woman.

And who is this in the picture?

That's my girlfriend, Moore said. No. That was my girlfriend. Not anymore, though. I forgot I still had that picture in my wallet.

What was her name? the Woodsman asked.

Rosemary.

Did you go with her a long time? the Woodsman asked.

Two and a half years or so.

And then it was over?

Yes.

Why?

I don't know.

Did you love her or she you?

She loved me first, Moore said. She saw that I loved her and told me so before I even knew I loved her myself. I wish I had known I loved her sooner. As it turns out, when I finally realized I loved her it was too late. There was already water under the bridge. We'd been broken up for a year and then it hit me boom just like that. I was sitting in one of these airports and I realized I had loved her all along, but it was too late. I had lost contact with her. I wouldn't know how to find her even if I tried. What's more, I've come to realize that if she wanted to be found she would let me know. None of my contact information has changed since she left.

The Woodsman listened intently trying to understand. He put the items back in the wallet and handed it back to Moore.

Now come on, the Woodsman said. Let's go. I want to show you something. Hiyya!

chapter 18
cumulonimbus pileus

They took off again through the woods and in the shadows up
ahead, darting in and out through the trees, was that large antlered
animal. At another part of the stream the Woodsman leaped over in
one bound—it was a wide crossing—and then he paused and with
his hand out he helped Moore across the stream. The antlered animal was standing off to the side observing. They—the Woodsman,
Moore, and the antlered animal—walked quietly through an ancient
forest that stirred Moore's heart like nothing he had ever before
experienced.

Moore kept saying, I am a six.

He didn't know what that meant, but it reminded him that he was
a human, an iteration, a numeric addition to the group humanity:
he was among the living. This was his moment with all these others.
Soon the moment would be over and a new generation of survivors
would supplant this one and they would have their own experiences,
and someone out there in the distant future might even find himself
running in a make-believe woods—and he too might even say I am
a six and not know what it meant, but that person might feel that he
too was an iteration of an endless repetition. And by so doing, there
would be an eternal linking through the generations and the word

"six" would echo in its own inscrutable way signifying what Moore and others out there just like him and yet to be born might never divine.

Still, Moore couldn't believe he was this close to the Woodsman nor could he believe he was walking through this ancient grove of woods. At one point he stopped walking and stared up at the tree-tops. The trunks of the trees were unbelievably thick and they rose to an incredible height.

Moore looked up and turned so the tops of the trees spun in the upper distance. My oh my, he said. I had no idea there were trees like this.

There aren't trees like this anymore, the Woodsman said. But there used to be. We cut them all down. Even I am to blame. I cut down my fair share in my day and I run more logs down the river than you can shake a stick at and I'm one who actually loves a tree. I wouldn't cut one down if I didn't have to. And when I cut heaving the long saw, and the tree falls onto the forest floor, I feel it break in my own heart. But what can you do? I'll tell you, though, what I have done. I've worked with the owner of this company, a crazy old Frenchman named Michel Tremblay, and I told him he can work me to death for a salary lower than most wages if he just let me have one hundred acres of trees and so he gave me this. Look around you, my friend, at the wonder of these uncut beauties.

What I ran through seemed more than this, Moore observed.

I'm bound in a pretty tight nut if that's what you mean, the Woodsman said, but I make the most of it, I do. When I first arrived here seven years ago much of this country stretched as far as the eye could see untouched. Now it is what it is, and I have this as a reminder of what it was. Now if you'll follow me here. This tree right here, I've nicknamed it Tiny. It's the tallest one on the property. Look up at the boughs. What do you see?

Moore looked up into the boughs of the tree and scrunched his eyes together because he saw something but wasn't certain what it

86

was he saw and then it came to him. A house, Moore said a moment later.

That's right. A house. My home. Now let's you and I go up into it. It's the most marvelous home in the world and I designed it myself. What we need to do is pull ourselves up by these ropes here. I've attached a series of pulleys to the uppermost limbs, and if you sit on one of these chairs and pull your weight, slowly you'll ratchet yourself up into the treetops. See? Watch how I do it and follow me.

The Woodsman got onto his swing-chair and started pulling himself up hand over hand and he ascended quickly.

Moore looked up at the elaborate pulley system to make sure it was secure.

Do you think you can do it? Do you think you have the strength? the Woodsman asked. A guy like you? Surely this will be a challenge that may be too great for you. But don't worry, should you not find the strength I'll help you out. I was made for such work. Now here. Before you go. Try these gloves on. They may help.

With that Moore consented. He slipped the work gloves onto his hands. They were made of calfskin, and the palms of the gloves had pine resin rubbed into them for gription. Moore sat on a piece of wood tied as a seat at the end of the rope. He reached, grabbed the hemp rope, and began to pull down on the rope with all of his strength and he heard the pulley system squeak and come to life. With each pull, he felt himself move incrementally upward. At first it was not very difficult pulling himself, but after a minute or two he was winded and he thought his arms would fall off from exertion. The Woodsman laughed.

I suppose you do a sort of work where you don't need your muscles, the Woodsman said. It must be a nice work, but it won't help you out none in the wilderness. Out here you'll find survival mostly depends on good reflexes, strength, and quick-wittedness. None of which you seem to have. No matter. There must be other things you have that are valued.

I can't think of anything myself, Moore puffed. Though I guess some people might call me a good salesman. For that all you need is to be attentive and listen. You have to know how to listen and wait for your moment to show how you might be able to help with your product. And if you do it in a seamless enough manner they don't even realize you're selling to them. They just think they're having a pleasant conversation with you.

The guy down at the lumber mill sells our logs, the Woodsman said. I suppose you could probably give him a run for the money. Show him a thing or two . . .

The fact is, Moore pointed out—and a salesman is always the first to speak in clichés—but the fact is: once a good salesman, always a good salesman. Or as another saying has it: the son of a cat always catches the mouse.

The Woodsman unexpectedly laughed.

What do you mean? the Woodsman asked.

I mean good salesmen are born, Moore said. My father was a salesman as was his father and for all I know his father all the way back through the family tree. We were all traveling salesmen of one stripe or another . . . drummers if you will. You don't make a salesman. You find them and it doesn't matter what they're selling or when they were selling, whether now or a few centuries ago. A good salesman is found and not made and he can sell you the air you breathe or the water you drink. You may be surprised to learn, Moore pointed out, that bottling water from streams more polluted than this one in a plastic bottle and selling it as bottled water is a multibillion-dollar-a-year business. And your guy down at the lumberyard is probably great-grandfather to the man who figured out how to sell water to a nation of joggers, commuters, and officegoers.

He probably was, the Woodsman agreed. But if you pulled on that rope more than you talked you might actually get somewhere.

See. That's another thing about a salesman that you have to watch out for, Woodsman, Moore said. You give him a small opportunity to talk and he's off to the races!

Gee, don't I know that. Now why don't you pull, because I'm sure as heck not going to help you at this rate.

Moore pulled himself hand-over-hand and he thought of the sadness of it: of never using his muscles but in the hotel gym. *These damned sinews were designed for physical labor and the best I can do with them is lift weight at the gym!* He pulled and up he went a little at a time, the pulley system creaking, moaning, but doing its job. With time, Moore found himself high above the ground, dizzyingly so, and yet he was only at the first boughs of the great tree.

The giant tree limbs spread out from the central trunk. They were thick and craggy but they were somehow welcoming. As Moore pulled he slowly rose above the limbs, one at a time. It was hard work, but it was good work. Occasionally, Moore looked through the thick branches and they seemed interwoven and interlocked like the fingers of a hand—a multifingered hand—and up he pulled, scaling up through the limbs interwoven like fingers, and looking down at the notches and clefts below it was as if he were looking down upon the palms of open and opening hands: they were the palms of the hands that might catch him should his rope break free from the pulley system and he fall.

Moore felt a mite and absurdly insignificant when measured against the scale of this mighty verdant tree. The Woodsman plied ahead of him, pulling himself rapidly and with the greatest of ease, and periodically he called down to make sure Moore was doing okay.

Hiyya! You okay down there? The Woodsman's voice echoed through the tenebrous wood.

I'm fine, Moore said. Better than I thought possible under the conditions.

A few hundred feet more and we'll be there.

As Moore advanced into the treetop he worked his way through the cloud cover. The clouds blocked his view of the surrounding region, and Moore felt as if he were lost in a fog. Clearly, he thought, this is a cumulus maximus that I'm pulling myself through. Moore pulled and pulled through the deep gray of the fog, and after a while he was up above the clouds in a blue celestial brightness. The great drama of the clouds exploding all around him filled him with a great and inexpressible joy, and yet he wasn't on an airplane, he was still attached by rope and pulling himself up toward the top of the tree and just when he thought he could pull no more he felt a rough hand grasp his wrist and it pulled him up through a hatch in the bottom floor of a cabin that had been built in the tree.

Welcome, the Woodsman said. This is my home. Humble but high. *Land of sky-blue wa-aters* is what I named her. I built it myself from logs I cut down and hewed. Hand over hand, I hauled them up one at a time and built my house.

I built it after my dog, Britt, died. He was attacked and eaten by a pack of wolves but he gave good fight, I tell you. He was a good dog and when he died I was so forlorn and lonesome I decided to move myself back where I always felt I belonged. High up here in the treetop with my own little section of forest down below.

And here I sit, like a saint or a holy man, although I am neither, I tell you. I like women too much. At least I like this one whore in town, a lady filled with sport when I show up on payday, and I don't suppose that puts me into the category of saint or holy man. Nevertheless, I've become rather a solitary sort. I look out over the cloud cover and I try to see if I recognize any faces in the clouds.

Often, I do see people I know from my past life. I see my mother and father. I talk to them, and often I see as big as a cloud my own dog, Britt, and would you believe he's always bounding off after one rabbit or fox or another. It's quite humorous watching the old boy who has become a cloud! It ain't much of a living up here. That I'll confess. But it does just fine by me. It makes me smile, anyhow. If that's what you're wondering?

chapter 19
cumulonimbus praecipitatio

Can Michel Tremblay.
Can Michel Tremblay?
Michel Tremblay.
Can Michel Tremblay please come to gate seventeen?
Please come to gate seventeen . . .
Michel Tremblay . . .

Moore opened his eyes and he sneezed, *Dsfasdkl;fasdfkjfdsakj* . . . He sneezed two more times, *Dsfasdkl;fasdfkjfdsakj* . . . *Dsfasdkl;fasdfkjfdsakj* . . .

A tendril of mucus dangled embarrassingly from the tip of his nose. Moore quickly pulled a handkerchief out of his pocket and blew his nose. He looked around to see if anyone at the gate noticed. It appeared unlikely. Folks around him were too distracted by their devices or they were bored out of their skulls and couldn't care less or they were stinking the place up with their containers of fast food and stinky socks.

Moore yawned.

He stretched.

91

He looked at his watch.

It had been four hours since this all started.

He couldn't believe he'd already been sitting here for four hours with no end in sight. The blizzard was pummeling the tarmac as hard now as when the storm started. It was nearly a whiteout out there. He saw in the gloaming the yellow-orange flashing light of a plow as it attempted to push back against the storm. Moore was thirsty. He had nodded off and he had been dreaming of something mildly pleasant though what it was, he couldn't say. He had a hard time remembering his dreams. Moore looked ahead of him at the crowd gathered at the gate and he thought: *I am a six.* Just then Moore noticed a priest in a collar staring at him.

Moore hadn't noticed the priest before. The priest sat two rows over and was staring right at him. *What's a priest doing here and staring at me for? A priest on a plane? I've never been on a plane with a priest before. Is it a bad omen? Surely it must be a bad omen, what other kind of omen could it be? A good omen?* There was no such thing as a good omen, was there? Just the word "omen" suggested menace, danger. There was the good priest, and yet in this context, in the context of the airport, the potentiality that he might be on the same plane as Moore—there was nothing good about him. He had become an omen. It was obviously an omen. *Should I be scared?* Moore was scared. Not very scared, just slightly.

On the other hand, just because one's scared and one feels there's some sort of ominous threat out there in the world doesn't mean it is a fact or that it is real. One's feeling about reality and reality itself are often two wildly different things. *That's a thought for you,* Moore thought. *Just keep that in mind. Go ahead, be a little scared because the priest is staring at you, but don't worry. Everything will be okay. Reality doesn't care two cents about whether a priest is on the plane or not. Priests have to fly, after all, don't they? They're people too, aren't they? You don't think they just stay holed up in their churches or their priest's rooms all day, do you? They're people just like us with families and errands that force them to travel.*

92

Moore folded the handkerchief and replaced it in his pocket. He tried crossing his legs again, but it seemed silly: there wasn't room for this sort of thing and more to the point he wasn't a meditator. Meditation was something, he thought, probably made sense. He believed it probably did increase one's inner peace. But it wasn't peace Moore was searching for. He had other things on his mind.

Like what? What other things do I have on my mind?

Moore closed his eyes again and tried to search for some definitive item he might find in his mind, but his mind was blank. *I'm a blank slate,* he thought. *My mind is blank too. There's nothing in it because there's too much traveling and too many airport acronyms on my itinerary.*

Last week alone Moore was in Fort Worth (DFW), San Jose (SJC), Seattle (SEA), and Boston (BOS). This forthcoming week, it was back to Cleveland (CLE), then up to Buffalo (BUF), and finally home to Chicago (ORD). The week after that it was Indianapolis (IND) for three days, followed by a two-day sales call to Fargo (FAR). After that Boston (BOS), then down to Miami (MIA) with a connection through Atlanta (ATL). When he finished Miami (MIA), he returned to Chicago (ORD) for a few days. After Chicago (ORD) it was back to Cleveland (CLE), then off to St. Louis (STL). From St. Louis (STL) he headed to Fort Worth (DFW) again and from Fort Worth (DFW) he was back in Florida, this time to Orlando (MCO). After Orlando (MCO) he went back to Boston (BOS). From Boston (BOS) he was scheduled to go to Toronto (YYZ) with a quick stop through Fargo (FAR), then on up to Winnipeg (YWG), and then from Winnipeg (YWG) he went on to Banff (YBA), which he had agreed to six months ago because a colleague of his was giving a training session to a group of associates. The subject of the talk, coincidentally, was "How to consolidate your sales territory, without losing sales presence." From Banff (YBA) he would head on down to Seattle (SEA); from Seattle (SEA) he was slated to go to San Jose (SJC); from San Jose (SJC) to Fargo (FAR); and after Fargo (FAR) it was back home to Chicago, this time through Midway (MDW), which would require a long late-night commute home.

It was too much territory for one man to cover but he couldn't say no. It was who he was—this territory, the way it extended across the country, was he.

If his boss asked if he'd like to go on a new sales call to expand his territory—to Minneapolis–St. Paul (MSP), let's say, or to Hartford, Connecticut (BDL)—he immediately agreed. At some point, Moore realized it didn't matter. His job was about striking out and finding new partnerships. That was what he signed on for when he signed on at Sonnenshein & Sons and that was what he'd do. It was who he was. It was a monastic existence, like that priest's!

His boss, Harvey, merely sat in the office day after day. A sedentary man slightly overweight, he pointed his finger to the green hills and told Moore to go, strike out, follow leads, discover new connections.

Besides, Harvey Sonnenshein liked to say, I don't fly. Never have. Never will. I'm superstitious of planes. Terrified of them. No, I won't take pills or drink alcohol to ease my fear of flying. Instead I'll make you go. That's why I hired you, Moore. If I could do it myself I would happily do so, believe me what it costs to send you scurrying about!

chapter 20
cumulonimbus spissatus

Moore felt packed in—it came with the turning of a moment
where after so long a wait he felt a downward shift in attitude, a terrible feeling, but one, unfortunately, he was used to—all this traveling. Maybe there was something to his father's theories of barometric pressure, and now he almost felt as if the pressure were bearing
down on him. He stood up and stretched, raising his arms high up in
the air. He stood on his toes. He tilted his head back and forth like a
prizefighter just before the bell. He yawned for oxygen and frowned.
What a day, he thought. He tucked his shirt in and shifted the
tension off his crotch. The snow was falling on the tarmac as the daylight, a pale and diminishing gray, gave way to an ever-diminishing
gray. He felt his stomach rumble and considered whether or not
to eat.

One part of him hated to get up from where he sat. The gate was
overcrowded; the crowds had migrated over to the neighboring gate.
Another part of him wanted to walk around, get the blood circulat-
ing. He sat down and thought about it.

I'm a hollow person, Moore thought. *I don't have anything inside me.*
He couldn't decide if such thoughts were pretentious or not. On
the other hand, he couldn't help having them. He knew if he looked

closely, such expressions would prove hollow; not he. Yet he had these thoughts all the time.

I'm hollow.

He never said it as if he meant it; he merely iterated it mindlessly as if it were some pointless mantra. If it were a jingle—it would be his jingle. In the mornings while his brain was still recompositing after a night of on-again, off-again REM sleep, he said the word "hollow" in a singsong voice. He muttered it: hollow hollow hollow.

What's hollow?

The tree is hollow.

What's hollow?

Balsa wood is hollow.

Is balsa wood hollow? Moore wondered. What is balsa wood? Something to make model airplanes with.

Airplanes are hollow and so are airports.

Moore looked around him at the gate. He was hollow and so was everyone else. The airport was hollow. It was a nice airport, he thought. It was attractive, clean. The architecture was steel and glass—with a lovely hint of airport modernism. It wasn't so bad, this airport. Aesthetically Moore liked it. What was bad about this particular airport—and all airports for that matter—was that it was a public place fraught with either a terrible sense of anxiety or its pair, terrible boredom.

Anxiety was one pole, boredom the other.

Positive/negative. AC/DC.

Only there was nothing positive about this, sitting here in a crowd of people, luggage strewn about the place. Across from Moore was that mom who kept chattering on her phone oblivious to everyone around her including her kid or kids. Did that boy really belong to the man reading the *Wall Street Journal*? It seemed unlikely, but maybe so. She kept chatting as if she were in the privacy of her own home and Moore thought to catch her eye again, but no doing. He glanced away and out the window toward the snow.

96

That's the problem, Moore thought, with all of this. No one has any time to be home anymore, and so the home has to be, perforce, brought into the public space. The evidence was everywhere to be seen.

Moore liked that word, "perforce," and he used it often while talking to clients: If you perforce try their product you will see that it is both more expensive in the long run and less effective than ours. That's why we have been in this business for seventy-five years, longer than any other company!

For the air traveler, the airport and the airplane functioned as stand-ins for the home, and when one was marooned at the airport one sought the amenities of home. Was the airport clean? Were the restrooms well maintained? Were the food basics easily obtainable, and could one proceed to the gate with a minimum of fuss feeling like they were still occupying a reasonably safe and pleasing space? And though airports worked hard trying to create the illusion that all these things were being taken care of, the fact was that an inveterate traveler saw all too easily not only the effort that the airport authorities put into the illusion but also how far short they fell and it didn't take too long before one felt acutely how impersonal and shabby these spaces really were.

Hotels and motels were no different, of course. No matter what effort was put into keeping them clean nor how thoughtful the interior accents were—the artful pictures that were hung on the wall, the comfortable chair pushed up in the corner with a pleasing reading lamp, the generous goose-down pillows and comforters that were turned down by the maid at night—Moore still couldn't escape the sense that it was all an illusion of home, nor could he let go of the idea that these rooms were every bit as publicly trodden and foot-worn as the airport terminal he lived most of his time in by day. The bed that he tucked himself into at night was only slightly less used than the airport chairs over there that the boy and the girl romantically slung themselves in.

Moore was homesick all of a sudden. *I travel too much. I'm never going to get ahead with all this traveling. Who am I going to find and marry if I'm always on the road like a Wandering Jew or sailor or hobo or seagull or anything else that wanders? No place is home. All places are just places and there's no place like home. Just click your heels three times and say it again, there's no place like home with your own coffeepot and another pot to piss in that is all your own.*

What happened to that Woodsman? How shall I find him again? The Woodsman was here a moment ago and the home in the treetop was so close at hand. And then there was all the wandering around apparently in a rather confined space. It was the illusion of places in the wild, Moore observed: they seem either farther or closer at hand, but never just where you think they are. *Click your heels*, Moore thought. *That's all you need to do to pass the time.*

Moore sat back in Buddha position, strained his back slightly against the chair, closed his eyes, and tapped the heels of his Crocs three times; the spongy rubber heels made a solemn *thump thump thump.*

chapter 21
cumulonimbus velum

Moore hoped he'd make it to Chicago tonight, though with the weather conditions such as they were, snow and more snow, he worried.

He'd been held up many times in the past. He'd missed his flight several times even this past year—his batting percentage on this account wasn't bad, though. He figured he was ninety-five percent on time to the airport. Occasionally he showed up late. He had underestimated either the traffic and distance to the airport or the lines of people waiting to be processed at the ticket counter or the security gate. He didn't have any strategy for dealing with the long queues winding through the rope corrals: all the people gathered around like cattle at the gate waiting for the final destination.

He couldn't stand in a line these days without thinking from time to time of cattle at the slaughterhouse, and whenever he thought of cattle being rounded up for the final cull he was so saddened by the dire inhumanity of human toward beast he vowed to give up meat forever. On the other hand, the great machinery of animal death would occur with or without his participation and as long as he had cravings for hamburgers and steaks it didn't seem likely he would ever really forgo meat.

99

Moore had even dated one or two vegetarians in his life. He'd dated a teetotaler as well. This last category was the most difficult to get used to. Moore wasn't a heavy drinker but he liked to have a beer or two in the evening. He even liked wine—especially if he was expensing it—and Moore enjoyed a drop of whiskey. He feared whiskey, worried that he liked it too much, that it might loosen his tongue, and once loose who knows what things he might be capable of uttering. That being said, Moore liked a drop of whiskey and the idea of dating someone who didn't drink at all seemed to him like an untenable match.

He'll never forget someone he went on a date once who said she "forswore" alcohol—that was her exact word:

I forswear alcohol, she said.

What do you mean? Moore had asked her. They were at a restaurant on their first date and with wine list in hand he asked her what she preferred: a cabernet or a zinfandel?

To which she responded: I forswear alcohol.

Moore thought she was joking or that he had missed her meaning under the conditions of the strange locution.

You what?

I forswear.

You swear?

No. I forswear. They're two different words.

Okay, since I never heard anyone use that word "forswear," you'll have to excuse me.

Well, there you have it, she said. We won't be needing any wine this evening because of my forswearence.

Did she really say forswearence? Moore wondered. It's possible. She had said quite a few things in the brief time their tryst had lasted.

For instance, not long after she used the word "forswearence," she had asked Moore to "ball" her.

Excuse me? Moore asked.

They had been standing outside his car and he fumbled for the keys. They had just finished their dinner and he had had a couple of whiskeys. Under the conditions he didn't trust his ears. He worried he was hearing things that weren't being said. She stood next to him, her body pressed to his.

Moore remembers a warm west wind blowing against his cheek—it was the green air of spring—and against the opposing cheek was her cheek. She must have been on her toes for she was considerably shorter than he, if he remembers correctly. He looked down at her and caught her eye, looking askance at her, wondering if he'd heard what she said.

Yes, she said, grabbing him. You heard me. I want you to *ball* me.

You want me to *ball* you? Moore asked, looking at her and still fumbling for the keys. When he finally got the door open, she slid into her seat. Moore walked around the back of his car and couldn't decide whether to be happy about this latest, unexpected turn of events or whether to be frightened. *Who do I have on my hands here?* he wondered.

Who did he have on his hands?

Her name was Lucy. At least that was what she told him. He immediately nicknamed her Lucy-Looking-Girl. In retrospect it seems foolish to have named her that, but under the conditions—romantic love or more accurately sexual attraction—it was the best he could do to express how he felt about her.

Moore had met her at a club, La Jolie, just a couple of nights earlier. At that point she hadn't forsworn alcohol. She was every bit as drunk as he. It was long beyond midnight—they slouched together in a chair, their faces intimately close as they spoke above the music. People were crowded about the floor bumping into them. I like you, she was saying above the music and the noise of the people.

You what? Moore shouted back over the music, unable to grasp what was being said.

I like you because you seem to understand me.

I what?

You understand me.

It seemed impossible. He even said so.

101

Impossible.

No, it's true, she reassured him. He revisited this point several times in the ensuing years to try to make sense of it.

He understood her. And yet what did this understanding consist of? A willingness to stare unblinkingly into her eyes as she rattled on about one thing or another he couldn't possibly comprehend: partly because he was drunk, partly because he couldn't hear everything she was saying, partly because he flat-out didn't understand a word she was saying? Or did this understanding consist of his willingness to bend closely to her face—both of them strangers to each other, yet suddenly intimately close as if they had been together forever? She had even said: I feel like I've known you forever even though we just met. You remind me of Mickey Rourke.

Of who? He worried she'd said Mickey Mouse.

Mickey Rourke.

Who was Mickey Rourke? Moore searched his memory, and just as it failed she helped him.

Rumble Fish. You remind me of Mickey Rourke in the movie Rumble Fish. Have you seen this movie?

A waiter came by and deposited two more drinks on the table next to where they were sitting. Moore fished his wallet out for cash and went back to smiling at her.

Do you know this movie, Rumble Fish? It's my favorite movie.

As a matter of fact, Moore did know the movie and he told her so.

Yes. It's one of my favorite movies. Matt Dillon and . . .

Mickey Rourke! That's who you remind me of. You have something that he has. The way your eyes are hooded, the way you talk. You don't seem to care what goes on around you. You're a shaper of the situation you're in. Not a mere participant.

What?

Not a mere participant. I like that about you.

After this comment they started to make out. Why not? What did he have to lose? Or as he later told a colleague of his who was semi-interested in his personal life: You only live once, right? So when she told me I reminded her of Mickey Rourke what was I to do but kiss her?

I tried to act like that Rourke guy as much as possible. I found myself trying to think like him. What would Mickey Rourke do in a situation like this? It was crazy, but if that was my calling card with Lucy-Looking-Girl, then I was going to play the part as much as possible. So when we were sitting there, I asked myself: what would Mickey Rourke most likely do in a situation like this? And it was at that point I kissed her, right there in the club with all these people around. It was surreal.

Even so, at least in sober moments, Moore was never the type to enjoy public displays of affection. His comment upon seeing young lovers necking in a coffee shop or on a park bench was invariably *Find a hotel room*, or *Can't you at least do that in the privacy of your own car?*

Now that Moore was drunk, it was after midnight, and her brown eyes had beckoned him across an alcoholic haze, Moore thought why not participate in this act of public sexuality? He closed his eyes, put his face near hers. He inhaled her perfume, which was so lovely it nearly made him weep. *The wonders of womanhood*, Moore thought. Her hair was soft in his hands. He put his hand behind her head and drew her toward him. They dueled with their tongues and pressed lips. A moment later she was in his lap, and he was slumped back in the lounge chair frantically making out as if catching up for lost time.

The physical presence of her—the three-dimensional realness of her and of her own desire—was so close it was nearly overwhelming. Her nose poked him just beneath the eye and suddenly he was having a hard time breathing, but he kept his tongue in her mouth, feeling around, groping. A moment later he broke for air, and he was back at it again: she was clawing at his chest, her hand was trying to undo his zipper. He was trying to get a feel beneath her bra. Who knows how much time passed while they made out in the noisy club—a minute? an hour?—but it was as if he was born for the first time. He felt himself coming alive. He wanted to laugh.

103

A moment later—disbelief, terror—a friend was dragging her away and she was gone out the door. Rescued.

What just happened? Moore wondered. His lap was still warm from her body. The scent from her hair lingered in the small intimate space just beyond him. He felt the abrasions of her face on his face. He pulled a long dark strand of hair from his mouth and frowned. He looked around: the debris and chaos of the drunken night was manifest when the bartender turned the lights on and made the announcement, Last call, and people started streaming out. It all seemed so garish all of a sudden. Who was she? Why did she leave? Where had she gone?

A moment later, as if to buoy a sinking feeling brought on by her departure, there she was right there in front of him, a big smile, perfectly real again and with her phone number on a napkin.

Call me tomorrow, she said. She kissed him one more time—smashing her lips against his. He reached for her hair, smelled it again as if to remember her. He felt he was falling through a dark familiar space and she pulled herself away from him and was gone.

Now here Moore was with her on a date. And *I want you to ball me* was still rattling around in his brain. It wasn't entirely improbable she had really said it, he just couldn't believe he was the object of such a phrase. What sort of locution was that coming from a woman? Moore wondered. The dinner had been mediocre and he worried his breath smelled of garlic and whiskey.

Moore got in the car and no sooner did he sit in the car seat than they resumed the position they had found themselves in two nights earlier at the bar. She lifted her dress and straddled him—there was that weight of her again, and the feeling of a human with desires competing with his own.

Moore couldn't believe what was happening. It was a late spring night; the sun had gone down but there were still solar rays of magenta, lavender, and orange sparking on the rim of the horizon and inflaming the cumulonimbus velum cloud formations that were bursting overhead between the treetops. There was a changing of barometric pressure, to be sure, Moore thought, and it didn't bode well for all the furry animals who wanted to come out of their hutches. Details popped out at Moore like how green and shiny the maple leaves looked in the shadowed night of early spring. A red-winged blackbird perched in the notch of a tree twirred. A donut half-eaten and folded up in a Dunkin' Donuts napkin lay next to a garbage can. People passed by on the sidewalk and seemed not to notice, or if they did notice he tried not to notice them noticing him and what she was doing to him. If Moore had known this was how events would have unfolded, he would have planned it differently.

Moore tried to imagine Mickey Rourke in *Rumble Fish*. Who was this Mickey Rourke guy? And how strange all of a sudden that he should play Mickey Rourke in someone else's fantasy: a role for which he of all people seemed ill-suited, to say the least. But wasn't she also a part of his fantasy, even as he remembered her now waiting at the airport gate with snow falling on the tarmac?

Moore started to laugh. He couldn't fit himself into the strangeness of the situation any longer.

Moore remembers her yellow cotton skirt hiked up just over her waist and the curve of her hip bending into the deepening shadows of the car. She was kissing him and he just started laughing.

Moore tried to explain himself to her but with the laugh he stepped outside some role he had tried on and became himself again. He couldn't help but see the situation as comical, and with that, the erotic moment had passed. It was the whiskey, Moore thought. The damn whiskey!

Why are you laughing at me? she asked. Why? Why? What is so goddamned funny?

It was a reasonable question. Certainly Mickey Rourke would not have laughed in such a situation. Moore felt somehow as if he had disappointed her. In his imaginings—when he dreamed of being with a woman—he never imagined disappointment. But in his real life disappointment always lurked just around the corner. Disappointment was like the light that had been turned on at the bar just two nights earlier as the bartender announced last call. The diverted eye was redirected to the chaos and debris of the fallen objects all around; the veiled beauty of the world seemed in retreat.

Take me home immediately, she directed.

She adjusted her dress. She folded her arms and stared moodily out the window as he drove her the few miles back to her apartment. He had her phone number still. He would call her in a day or two to see if she'd like to give this one more try. In the meantime, he'd just keep his mouth shut. As he pulled up to her apartment, she quickly got out of his car and ran, little steps, in her heels to the gate of her complex. He noticed that she lived in the same fallen world as he and, with that, he drove away.

cumulonimbus tuba

When Moore opened his eyes in the airport a moment or two
later a pubescent boy, acne-stained, gangly, maybe all of fourteen
or fifteen years old, was standing before him with his hand out. It
startled Moore that someone was standing so close to him, and for
a moment he tried to focus his eyes to make out what this was all
about. The boy wanted something and he stood there in front of
Moore with an intention that was not quite beggarly, but solicitous.
His large teeth were imprisoned in braces and there it was, the boy
asked for a dollar. He was wearing a shirt that said:

ONLY THE PIMP
WEARS
THE GREEN SHIRT

In this case, the boy's shirt was green. What the hell does that
mean? Is it the name of a band? A song lyric? A statement of revolt?
"Only the pimp wears the green shirt" . . . Or a statement of fact?
Moore did his best not to show alarm, but he had been caught off
guard and he was disturbed by the boy's proximity. Moore looked
carefully at the boy, who seemed humorless, a bit dangerous, and
Moore wondered who was raising this child. Who could possibly

be raising a child wearing a shirt that essentially says by its green-
ness and its statement I am a pimp? Does a fourteen-year-old or
fifteen-year-old really know what a pimp is?

Moore looked at the boy and was half-tempted to ask him if he
indeed knew what a pimp was. More interesting, on second thought,
would be to discover whether the kid knew who the current president
was or could he, say, identify the fiftieth state? Moore imagined the
boy launched into the world with the label "pimp." Once labeled a
pimp where does one have to go but up? Was up possible unless it
was through some murky chain of command in the vast sprawling
alternate universe of gang life of which Moore knew next to nothing?

No, Moore said to the boy.

No, what?

No. I'm not giving you a dollar.

Please, the boy said.

He said please! Impossible to believe such a kid could be possessed of manners.

No.

Thank you anyway, sir. Have a nice day.

With that the boy was off.

Was it some sort of joke? A prank to send a boy to him asking him
for a dollar? Was the green shirt part of the prank?

Moore looked over to the man next to him who was reading the
Wall Street Journal. The man seemed not to have noticed the boy. He
was oblivious: locked in his own world of thought. The woman on
the phone, across from Moore, didn't seem to notice either.

Across from Moore the heavy man was snoring so much that his
goitrous throat moved in and out like a bellows. What was it that
woke you up in the middle of the night? Sleep apnea? Yes, Moore
thought. That man must be one of those who have sleep apnea.
Nearby was the priest staring out at the tarmac and thumbing (was
it nervously?) a rosary. Hail Mary full of grace. Blessed art thou
among women and blessed is the fruit of thy womb, Jesus . . .

108

Moore watched Pimp Boy trudge off. He didn't trudge exactly. No, he walked quite calmly and a little swiftly away. *The nerve of him,* Moore thought, *to stand like that and beg me for money.* Moore followed the boy with his eyes and watched him crossing the concourse until the boy disappeared into the men's room, which was kitty-corner and just down the way from the gate.

Moore kept his eye on the men's room entrance to wait for the boy to emerge. *He must be working for someone,* Moore thought. *There must be somebody putting that kid up to panhandling. Someone who makes him wear that offensive shirt as well. In this circumstance, who's the pimp?*

Moore wondered if he should report the kid to the airport authorities, but who were the airport authorities exactly? Moore hated the word "authority," and yet in cases like this shouldn't the authorities be consulted?

Moore wished that he were traveling with someone. This was a case—and Moore felt it more and more often these days—where he saw something that he wished he could share with someone. Only he never had anyone to share his observations with. *I wish,* Moore thought, *I had someone to travel with from time to time. All of this traveling alone and living alone is not healthy. Whom do I share my adventures and observations with? Worse, no one has committed to sharing their observations and intimate thoughts with me. It was too singular a life not to have someone to share it with.* Moore felt the poignancy of the loss—was it a loss if you never had it to begin with?—of not having a companion.

If he had a companion, he would lean over and secretly point the boy out. *What do you think that was all about? Why do you think he came up to me like that? Why was he wearing such a shirt? And what does it mean?*

ONLY THE PIMP
WEARS
THE GREEN SHIRT

Isn't it all so alarming? And his companion—he imagines a woman with a commensurate worldview, possibly his same age—agreeing with him on this point.

Yes, it is alarming, she might say. I wonder if we should consult the authorities.

I hate to consult the authorities, Moore would say. I never liked the authorities.

Nor have I, she might agree. Yet under the conditions, a boy running around with a shirt like that asking for money, it's disturbing to say the least.

I'll say.

Who knows? The boy disappeared into the men's room. Maybe he was soliciting sex? Maybe he's not the pimp. Maybe he's the prostitute.

Disturbing!

Yes.

Then why did he approach me? Moore might ask. Do I look like someone who would be interested in having sex with a boy? I don't think so!

Nor do I, she would agree. At this she might laugh. I don't see it either, but who knows what that kid is doing or seeing or why he picked you, Jim, to approach and not someone else.

Like that priest, for instance . . .

Yes, like the priest, she might say. There must be a reason he clutches that rosary so.

I thought it was because he was worried the plane might go down or praying that it might finally show up.

It may be, on the other hand, that the priest knows about the boy and he is praying for the strength to resist temptation.

Yes, Moore thought, the strength to resist temptation. Life was filled with temptation . . .

Just then, the boy emerged from the men's room. His hair appeared to have just been washed. It was wet and combed back.

His shirt was turned inside out. He strode over to the automatic walkway, and instead of getting on the walking surface, he jumped up on the handrail and rode it all the way to the end like a disenfranchised adolescent. When he got to the end he jumped off and rode the handrail back in the opposite direction. Occasionally he looked over at Moore and smiled. Moore found this more alarming than he could say. He dropped his head to his hands and tried to compose himself.

With my luck, I'll probably end up getting seated next to this miscreant. That's the problem with all this waiting, Moore thought. People get stir-crazy and when people get stir-crazy anything can happen.

chapter 23
cumulonimbus virga

Moore thought back to Rosemary. He smiled at the thought of her. *If she were here, she would be my companion. Her bad back would make this situation difficult, but still she would somehow laugh through the whole thing. It'd be interesting to know what she would make of all this. She was always filled with so many wonderful observations. It's too bad things never worked out between us.*

He now wishes that they had worked out. In retrospect, Moore thinks he liked her more than he thought he did at the time. *I was foolish to let her go. I didn't let her go, let's face it. She moved on because she saw better than I did that we were ultimately incompatible.*

We weren't incompatible, Moore thought. *We were a match. When we were in sync there was nothing like us. She even said so herself.*

She was fond of looking him in the eyes and telling him that she saw her own genetic past staring right back at her. You and I are more alike than you think, buster, she liked to say. We must have ancestors in common. We're part of the same tribe. I feel it in my bones when I'm with you, like I'm home at last.

He would smile and say, Au contraire.

What? You don't see it, she'd ask disappointed.

Moore could be flippant about her affections and how he fit into them because he didn't feel it—this bond—as strongly as she did and when he seemed most heartless she would very warmly, though sadly, push him away and say, It's too bad you don't see it, Jim. It's too bad you don't understand what *we* have here.

Moore never protested this. He didn't see the need, and his silence seemed to confirm a truth. She was right. He didn't understand, and it *was* too bad.

Moore understands now, though. Hell, he understands only too well that they had been meant for each other but that he had missed the boat on their relationship. *Was I born to be an idiot and miss it? What was I thinking? I felt so distracted at the time. What was I distracted by? I was distracted by her. I couldn't quite understand her energy level. She was so rich with emotion, so vibrant with laughter, so filled and bubbling over with stories.* Moore never got over the suspicion that he didn't merit her attentions. She was greatly beyond him in talent and emotion and one day, he was certain, she would come to understand that and from there everything would fall apart. But maybe it was he who had underestimated her.

Moore would like to contact her now and let her know that he finally gets it. They were compatible in a weird, though sensible way. He did feel the way she did, he was only slow to realize it. It was a time bomb that just took a little longer to go off for him than for her. She should understand that it might take him longer to get it. She always used to sigh because he was so damn cool, emotionally.

I don't get you, Jim, she would say. Her exasperation was real.

What don't you get? he would say. I'm as simple as a lightbulb.

Maybe one that is turned off or dead. But I wish sometimes you might turn on. Some light inside you . . .

Moore could contact her when he got back to Chicago and remind her of this conversation. He would tell her that he has finally turned on and now he gets it. They were meant for each other.

The obvious problem, though, is that Rosemary is too far gone from him . . . She's doubtless moved on to other cities, to other partners. She left and never looked back. Where was she now? Who was

113

she? Was she married? Did she have kids? She wanted kids. She was convinced that they would have beautiful kids. Where was she living? He had lost track. It was irresponsible to do so and now he wouldn't know how to find her even if he tried. It serves him right. They had ended their relationship just as he was expanding in the Southwest and this helped him to get beyond the emotional loss. It was nice to always be gone and not risk seeing her about in the neighborhood. One day he heard from someone, he doesn't remember who, that she had left for Brooklyn. That was the last he knew of her where-abouts. And frankly, she could be anywhere. Even Anchorage, Moore thought.

Now, with all the years of travel between them, he felt empty. *I'm hollow . . . I've become . . . My life is . . . I feel so . . .* "Useless" was the word that came to mind and it wasn't a jingle or a mantra. *I wish she were here by my side as I wait for my plane. I wish I could talk to her right now. Not just about that boy wearing the crazy shirt, but about so many things. I wish I could tell her about how my client's son Ricky has leukemia and how I'm contributing to his health care program. If Rosemary and I were together it would be a donation that could be made in both of our names.* Instead, Moore kept the donation anonymous. He didn't want his client to think that he was contributing to win over his business.

He had met Ricky one day on the golf course. He and his client were golfing and his client's son came along. It was a beautiful summer day. They were on a golf course overlooking the cape. Ricky was just growing his hair back after a go-around with chemo. He remembers Ricky being funny as hell. There were seagulls flying over the golf course and Ricky was making all sorts of jokes about the birds and leukemia. Death and dying and laughter were in the air that day. The kid seemed smart beyond his years. Moore and his client were laughing so hard at the kid's jokes that they couldn't finish eighteen under ninety. How old was that Ricky? No older than this one here with the pimp T-shirt.

Moore looked over at the kid riding the automatic walkway's handrail, but he was gone. Moved on to other stranded travelers. He didn't hold it against the kid that he was wearing the green shirt. It was merely a sign of the times. Pornography was everywhere. But my God, Moore would do anything in the world to see his client's son survive. He laughed at the thought of Ricky, then stared back at the woman talking on the cell phone. He was waiting . . . waiting for her eyes to lift.

On she droned.

chapter 24
altocumulus perlucidas

If Moore was lucky enough to sign in and get a low number in the queue to get on the plane, then he often had the luck of the empty seat. When he had the opportunity, he picked a seat near the front of the plane. First on, first off was his philosophy. He also thought it was a slightly quieter ride in front of the wings rather than behind them where there was so much draft and engine hum. Also, he didn't like the foot traffic to the toilet at the back end of the plane where lines of anxious people who waited to go to the bathroom tended to collect.

If, while boarding, Moore happened to find an emergency exit with extra legroom near row nine or ten, so much the better. He liked to claim an aisle seat so he could roam about in the aisle as needed once airborne. An aisle seat also gave him an opportunity to stretch his legs when the aisle was clear. Boarding early on the plane gave him ready access to the overhead bins. Once he settled in, Moore would intently watch the rest of the crowd from the gate usher onto the plane.

There was always a seat to the left or the right of him depending on which side of the plane he occupied, and he'd look carefully at the faces of the people boarding the plane trying to guess who in this lineup would sit down next to him. He was a big enough guy, broad in the shoulders with just the hint of an intimidating face, to discourage anyone from settling down next to him. And in fact, people didn't settle down next to him. Only after the plane became crowded and a call for filling last seats went out would someone ask if the seat next to him was available. Of course, it's available, suit yourself. But as often as not, the empty seat next to him would be the last empty seat to fill.

Moore never quite knew why he had the luck of the empty seat, but he suspected that his face with a natural scowl and the broad shoulders were part of it. *I'm mildly feared*, Moore thought. *Nothing wrong with that, certainly, especially if it provides me with a little extra space on the plane.*

If the space next to Moore was finally taken, the passenger invariably kept to themself. The days of social pleasantries on an airplane were long gone.

The same laws applied at the gate as well. Usually, no matter how crowded the gate, there was at least one seat available either to the left or the right of Moore. And today, despite the crowded gate and the long uncomfortable wait, the seat next to Moore had remained empty. Moore was grateful for this empty space, especially since the wait had been so long. Moore was against blocking seats with a bag or a jacket and he did nothing to deter fellow passengers from sitting next to him, but nevertheless this seat remained open and free. No one had even inquired about its availability. Moore thought to offer it to one elderly lady who was loaded down with luggage and looked as if she might drop dead any moment, but her scanning eye caught a free seat near the priest and she shuffled her luggage there.

The seat adjacent to the priest had probably remained open because he was a priest, or so Moore reasoned, and the gate was probably filled with more than a few lapsed Catholics who might be a bit shy of the priest, not to mention the certain number of folks that must harbor animosities toward the Church in the wake of the scandal and of its perverse and prolonged suppression of women from the priesthood. It was a terrible thing to witness—the isolation of the priest, the reduction of Church membership. In his youth, which played out in the final days of Vatican II, the Latin Mass was in its final decline but in some churches it was still being said, and priests were revered. He himself remembers being an altar boy—an acolyte—with red-and-white vestments. The goal was always to stay awake long enough to ring the bells at transubstantiation. *If only we could be transubstantiated, how wonderful that would be.* Moore would take his transubstantiation right now, without further ado, thank you very much.

It had been a fantasy of Moore's—being not just an angel but a fully incarnated angel renewed for everlasting life and rising on spires of pink-hued evening light toward some heaven that looked hardly different than one of those great altocumulus perlucidus cloud formations that veiled the sky like a grid of clouds and let the blueness of the sky or the whiteness of the moon or the light of the sun shine through the gap between the clouds. It beats this type of travel any day. No waiting around in airports. Oh, he'd probably be laughed at by the priest if he joked about being transubstantiated into a cloud. At the very least, he'd be shooed away.

That's what Moore remembers from his days as an acolyte: being shooed away by the priest when he attempted to peer into the church's golden tabernacle where the communion wafers and wine chalice were held. Body and Blood of Christ. Amen. The words still nearly trembled upon Moore's lips. In an act of reflexive memory, he bowed his head and nearly said a prayer. *What would I pray for at this point in time?* Moore wished he had something to pray for. Oh sure, he had plenty to pray for. Too much. That's why he wasn't sitting next to the priest. He felt guilty at all the years that had elapsed and still no confession, no amelioration of sin, no intercessor speaking on his

118

behalf to clear his soul. *One day I'll do that, though,* Moore thought. *I'll go to church—preferably one with a Latin Mass—*which, incidentally, he had read in *USA Today* was making a comeback in certain parishes. *I'll go to the Latin Mass. I'll confess my sins behind the closed doors of a traditional confessional. I'll light a votive candle for my maternal ancestors, I'll donate a large sum to a Catholic charity, and then I'll chant one or two times my own private cloud kaddish in remembrance of my old man . . .*

cumulus fractus, cumulus humilis, cumulus mediocris, cumulus congestus; stratocumulus castellanus, stratocumulus lenticularis, stratocumulus stratiformis; stratus fractus, stratus nebulosus, stratus opacus, stratus translucidus, stratus undulatus; cumulonimbus calvus, cumulonimbus capillatus, cumulonimbus incus, cumulonimbus mammatus, cumulonimbus pannus, cumulonimbus pileus, cumulonimbus praecipitatio, cumulonimbus spissatus, cumulonimbus velum, cumulonimbus tuba, cumulonimbus virga; altocumulus perlucidus; altostratus duplicatus; mammatus; altostratus nebulosus, altostratus opacus, altostratus pannus, altostratus praecipitatio, altostratus radiatus, altostratus translucidus, altostratus undulatus, altostratus virga; cirrostratus nebulosus; nimbostratus pannus, nimbostratus praecipitatio; cirrus castellanus; nimbostratus virga

What are my sins? Moore asked himself. My chief sin, he thought, must be that of hypocrisy. Moore remembers as a child reading all about hypocrites in the Gospels. He didn't understand what that word meant, nor who those persons—those hypocrites—were, but he understands what it means now. He understands all too well. *You can't run around smiling at people and being all rosy on the outside while thinking the thoughts I think, and not think yourself a hypocrite.* If not a deadly sin, hypocrisy was still high up on the chart. Forthwith, starting now, Moore would try harder not to be a hypocrite.

Moore watched the old lady, stumbling, shuffling off to the priest. Good for her, Moore thought. It must be some consolation to the priest as well to have that elderly woman sit down next to him in semblance of close confidentiality, almost supplication. She assumes the posture of a supplicant so that the priest mustn't feel so much a pariah with her by his side.

Too bad about that, Moore thought. About the priests and what's become of them, nowadays, always in the news for the wrong reasons—for closeted pedophilia and endless cover-ups. The old lady was so tired she looked as if she might drop her head on the priest's shoulder and expire. Instead, she merely yawned and stared blankly at her worn-out shoes. Moore noticed that her eyes were heavily mascaraed and she wore on her soft wrinkled cheeks a touch of powdered rouge.

The seat adjacent to Moore had remained vacant because of what he represented: a white male businessman. In this way, Moore was not unlike the priest, a sort of pariah. Others had warily eyed the seat next to him, but then, upon seeing Moore, they moved on to a different position at the gate. *It confirms my feeling again and again,* Moore thought. *I'm part of the business class, not to mention my size, my age, and my sex: I'm a man and an inheritor of implicit white male privilege and, as a result, I just naturally intimidate. Whatever the case may be, people refuse to fill the seat next to me. This is why I won't walk around the gate even though my bladder is starting to give me problems. I don't want to lose this empty space next to me. It's an unasked-for perk that comes with type. How else to explain it?*

Moore looked around him and saw everybody else suffering in the overcrowded space. No one had any elbow room, but Moore did and he'd like to retain it as long as possible. He hoped the planes would start running. It wasn't clear how much longer the wait might be. Moore wondered how long he could hold off until a bathroom break. He shouldn't have had that large coffee. He was dehydrated too, and if he remained dehydrated too long a headache might follow. Moore hated being underhydrated and yet airports just seemed to dry him out. It was a terrible thing what the air in airports did to him. More often than not it made him sick, or if not sick, ill-tempered.

chapter 25
altostratus duplicatus

Just as Moore was starting to feel gratitude for the empty seat next to him, a woman threw her bags on the ground near his feet. The baggage bumped his leg and forced him to reorient his position on the seat. Moore felt compromised. *This is where it all starts. Compromise here and it's all downhill. Before you know it you'll be a pretzel twisted in a space that's already too small for a natural-grown man.*

Moore nudged the bags slightly so they wouldn't intrude into his zone and lifted his eyes to the perpetrator.

Excuse me, she said. She had walked in as if in a hurry and was all out of breath—though Moore could swear he had just seen her a moment ago sitting on the floor near the other end of the gate. She was very tall, almost stately—why are women "stately," Moore wondered, and men just tall? And yet, looking up at her, sensing a force greater than himself, he couldn't quantify her size any more appropriately. She threw her hair back and sat down next to him with an *oomph*.

She was wrapped up in a parka. She was wearing Ugg boots. He never liked the things and he thought they were only half appropriately named. She wore her elastic hair band around her wrist, and she started flicking her hair out of her face and throwing it back.

When she shifted in her seat and bumped into him, he glanced briefly at her expecting some apology, but none was offered. She immediately put herself in lotus position—her legs crossed, her hands balanced on her knees palm upward, the thumb and index finger touching, the fingers forming an O. After a moment, she turned and smiled at him.

I saw you trying to do yoga. I do yoga too, she said.

I was doing yoga? Moore blurted. When was I doing yoga?

A moment ago I saw you.

Oh, come off it.

You were! You know I'm right! the stately woman said.

Moore looked quickly at the woman staring at her phone across from him and worried what she would think of this. On the other hand, why did he care what she thought. As of yet, she hadn't even lifted her head to notice him. Moore tried to be as brief and dismissive of the woman in yoga position as possible.

You aren't right. You're wrong, he said.

You need to work on your flexibility, though, she told him.

I wasn't doing yoga.

You had your legs crossed and your hands were on your knees. We call that half lotus.

You're kidding, right? Moore asked.

No. I believe you're kidding me, she said. The way you tried to fold your feet into your lap is yoga.

I was only doing that, Moore said, because of the cramped quarters, not because I'm some sort of Yogaist. For a moment Moore debated if he should tell her he clicked his Crocs three times and said: There's no place like home.

You don't have to be a Yogaist to practice yoga, she informed him.

Well, I wasn't practicing yoga.

I saw you.

Hmph.

I noticed you doing mountain pose. You were doing it crudely, she said, but you were doing it.

123

I was doing no such thing, Moore said.

I was sitting right over there watching you in broad daylight, she said. You put your hands on your hips, then you reached for the sun. Only you can improve your method. Here let me show you how. I'm not an expert, but here. Stand up.

No thank you, Moore said.

Please stand up. Don't ignore me. Do as I say. She removed her parka. She was wearing a T-shirt underneath. On the T-shirt was the silhouette of a mountain and of a man climbing it. It reminded Moore of the Woodsman. How uncanny, he thought. Does she know what I'm thinking to be wearing a T-shirt like that? The stately woman smiled at him and offered her hand. Please stand up. Let me show you how to get more from your mountain pose. She reached for his hand, and as soon as he felt her hand in his, he didn't know what else to do. Something inside him that had been rigid for a very long time yielded. He smiled at her and did as she said: he got up.

Thank you, he said.

Don't thank me until you do this.

Okay. I'm ready.

Here, watch me.

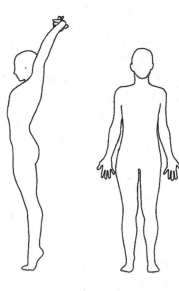

124

chapter 26
mammatus

They stood there a moment. She said as if not speaking merely to him but performing for the whole terminal, This is how you do mountain pose. The woman sitting across from Moore stopped talking on her phone and looked up at them skeptically. Moore felt his heart sink.

The Yogaist went on: Now close your eyes and just listen. I'm going to narrate the story. You follow along. Here goes:

You are standing on a branch. Perhaps you are a young bird with new feathers and the green world with its dandelions and clover and wild mysterious smells beckons. Close your eyes and I will narrate exactly what you see next.

Tweet, Moore said.

Stop that and pay attention to me.

The forest smells . . .

Please pay attention, she said.

Moore tried not to pay attention. He was too frightened to pay attention. *What will everyone think of me now standing here like a fool? Doing what some crazy woman is telling me to do. Hey wait. Wasn't she just sitting over there against that wall a moment ago? What's she doing standing by me? I'll call the authorities!*

Okay, she said, in a brave voice: mountain pose. Put your hands on your hips, please.

Moore was impressed with how direct and . . . stately she was in this pose. He put his hands on his hips in emulation.

Heels together, she said.

Moore put his heels together.

Toes out.

Is this ballet or yoga? Moore asked.

Good question. Most men wouldn't think to ask that. Let me guess, you have a daughter?

No, I don't. I'm single.

Good. But to your question: looked at from one angle, ballet and yoga aren't all that different from each other but, from another, there are immensities between them. If this were ballet we'd be in first position. But this is mountain pose. Remember, we're doing yoga.

Heels together, toes out. I'm in first position for mountain pose.

Good. Now hold it.

When do we get to do ballet?

Next time. Now close your eyes for this.

Moore stood next to her, glanced at her, and she was staring back at him patiently waiting for him to close his eyes.

Okay, close your eyes, please . . .

In my time, Moore muttered. In my time . . .

Before Moore did so, he scanned the gate. He noticed a man and a woman dressed in the uniforms of airline staff step behind the check-in counter. How did one do a job like that day after day? Moore wondered. There must be some clique of airport workers, a society of friends; camaraderie in this business that helps make these airport jobs endurable. If you worked in an airport there must be places where you went to unwind with other airport staff. He hoped those places weren't in airports but feared for airport workers that they might be—the one or two cantinas scattered through airports serving margaritas and beer.

126

Moore spent so much time in airports around these workers and yet he knew next to nothing about them. Airport workers were essentially invisible to him, just as he must be invisible to them. Moore hoped he was invisible, that he passed unnoticed. He always aimed to be unobtrusive. It wasn't modesty; it was something closer to the humility he felt in the presence of others involved in their own work tasks. The two airline staff members were shuffling through some papers. Moore hoped it meant that there would be an announcement any moment of an impending departure so he could end his yoga lesson with this woman.

Close your eyes so you won't be distracted, she said. Please, if you want to do this right, you have to listen to me.

Without further ado, Moore did as he was told by the Yogaist, and he waited for an announcement that flights would resume any minute. Moore was tired; he wanted to go home.

Moore's eyes were closed and he worried that again he would be asked to fall into himself, falling into himself to recount some miraculous moment that never happened in his forgotten childhood on a miserable, mostly fallow scrap of land called his childhood home in Iowa. He worried that he would be asked to let go—and the worry wasn't so much that he'd be asked, but that he would disappoint her when he said no. We are too soon together for disappointment to intrude. But sooner or later it always did, didn't it?

Who am I? Moore wondered. He stood vertical in an inviolate space, his eyes shut to the world. He was listening to a woman he didn't know and all the ambient noise of the airport surrounded him. *Who am I and what am I doing acting like a fool in front of all these people? Be humble, and considerate. That's the only way to be,* Moore thought. *We are here but briefly and then we are gone. No need to stir the pot more than it needs to be stirred.*

What if a customer of mine should appear at the gate and see me standing here with my eyes shut preparing for mountain pose or first position or whatever it is she's trying to teach me? What if others at this gate saw me like this: how could they not suspect me of terrorism, or of collusion with a terrorist; how could they not look and worry that a malleable lunatic was in their midst?

Is she a terrorist? Of course she isn't. Wait, maybe she is. I'm terrified, Moore thought. He felt a tingle of fear ripple through his body. He couldn't identify the source of the fear exactly but it was a combination of her and of him doing something not only out of character but completely mad. *If I were in my right mind I would tell her to go to hell, but it's desperation making me do this. Desperation, loneliness, and what???*

What is it that makes me obey her? He was intrigued. *Why not listen? Why let the setting of this gloomy place tamp you down? Follow your instincts . . .*

Her voice is intimate. It speaks close to the lobe of his ear. Moore feels the vibrations of her voice in the small hairs of his ear: *You see a bird in flight,* she whispers. *A moment ago the bird had been perched on a branch right next to you. Are you with me?*

Yes, Moore said.

Good, she said. Keep your eyes shut and follow me with your mind. Now to continue . . . *You hear the bird's wings flap, and before you know it, it's off through the green maze of leafy branches flying. You follow the bird with your eyes, and you can, because it's a red-winged blackbird. You follow the little blotches of red on its wing as it flies off into the green shadows of the forest. You watch it fly away and feel panic. You panic because the bird flying away from the nest is your mother. You don't know if she'll ever come back. There was something about the way she lured you out to the branch, then took off without feeding you a worm. Why did she lure you out without feeding you a worm? You're too hungry. You start to scream for her and your voice comes out a chitter: a twirrr. You are a bird. Your wings are your arms; your hands are on your hips. Now it's your turn to try to fly after. You raise your wings over your head and reach for the open space beyond. You don't know that she's not going to return but there's something about the way she left the nest encouraging you to step out on the branch with her—the ground, a tangle of growth and shrubs is far below. Your instincts tell you that*

128

if you don't venture forth she'll be gone forever. You take off and as you fall you feel lift beneath your wings. It's a miracle that you don't fall but gather the wind beneath your wings and fly. You move your wings again and dart toward the open spaces ahead. Your reflexes are sharper than you imagined, navigating with sudden twists and dips, through the woods, avoiding the branches and leaves. You follow your heart and find yourself in an open clearing and you land on the ground.

Wow that was fun, you think. That was the most wonderful, the most exciting thing you've ever experienced and you're just a young bird. How wonderful to be a bird. The first day of flight. It's like discovering gold. What fortune—this flight! What joy lies ahead!

She interrupts: I know this is yoga. I know you're supposed to clear your mind and all that. But I always say if I'm going to meditate I'm going to do it my way. I like to tell myself stories. Most often I imagine I'm in some crazy wilderness. Today, we just happened to be red-winged blackbirds taking off on our first day of flight. Wasn't that fun? If you look across the grassy field you'll see me watching you. Tweet.

Tweet, Moore said back to her.

Moore lowered his arms to his side and sighed. It was a happy sigh. He felt mildly exhilarated. Not by the yoga, but by the company of this woman.

Wasn't it fun? she asked.

It was fun, Moore said. I felt I was a bird flying. What could possibly be more fun?

Moore opened his eyes and smiled brightly at her. He felt strange, but he felt okay with feeling strange.

Now you can thank me, the Yogaist said.

Thank you, Moore said. Thank you for getting me to move around and to stretch my wings.

You're welcome.

Do you feel better now?

I do.

Tweet.

Tweet.

chapter 27
altostratus nebulosus

It was strange. Moore was happy all of a sudden. He felt joy in his heart. A smile was breaking across his face. It amazed him how accidentally and suddenly joy could grab hold of him. It was always around a woman, he thought. Not any kind of woman, usually it was with a woman who was more attractive than he thought he deserved but who nonetheless seemed keenly interested in him. He wondered if that could pass as his definition of happiness.

Moore thought of Immanuel Kant and of his *Foundations of the Metaphysics of Morals*, which he was required to read as a college student. It had been difficult to understand that book. Moore broke his head trying to make sense of it. In the end, what Moore walked away with was this simple phrase: "Treat no person as a means to an end, but an end in themselves." It seemed an unattainable moral standard and frankly Moore didn't know what the hell it had to do with happiness. Moore liked his definition better. It seemed more to the point and descriptive of the joy and cruelty he would discover in his life and it went something like this: "Happiness is a woman prettier than you deserve who nonetheless takes a keen though fleeting interest in you."

He remembers one woman, her name was Leanne. It hurt him now just to remember her name. She had given him happiness but cruelty was somehow wrapped up in his meeting with her. Moore met Leanne while he was going with Rosemary and their brief affair ended his relationship with Rosemary. Moore had never betrayed a relationship before but Leanne somehow sensed his weakness and targeted him. That was the way he explained it but Rosemary wasn't buying it.

Tell me the truth about what happened.

Nothing happened.

Tell me, please, the truth. Only the truth will save you.

Moore looked at her and in the most urgent sincere tones he could muster, he said: nothing happened.

Her back had been bothering her that day. She asked him to leave. She needed to lie down and try to get this back pain under control.

Can I come back later? Moore asked. Can we talk?

We can talk all you want, Jim. You seem good at talking. You do it oh so well.

As he walked out of Rosemary's apartment, Moore thought of that fateful afternoon he had with Leanne . . .

On that afternoon, Moore sat in Leanne's bathroom as she applied makeup. She wasn't wearing clothes and she said under her breath: The only reason why you're here, Jim, is because you want to fuck me.

I missed that. What did you say? Moore said.

Hmph. You know it's true.

No . . .

Yes it is.

Moore denied it, but she was right. He had spent weeks working with her, desiring her—and then suddenly, this had come about.

It all happened in a moment. Leanne called him one day to come over. She wanted to talk. She also needed some things moved around her apartment and would you mind helping?

132

Of course not, Moore said on the phone. I'd be happy to help.

With her address in hand, Moore sped across town hardly believing his luck, half-worried that all she wanted to do was talk and to use him as her own personal helper.

She needed some chairs moved from her basement locker onto her back porch. Moore carried them up for her, dusted them off, and cleaned them. She also asked him if he would mind installing an air conditioner. Moore obliged her in this as well, carrying the heavy machine up from the basement, breaking a sweat, struggling to install it in her window. Also, Jim, would you mind moving my couch so we can put the table there? Leanne pointed and Moore moved the couch. Moore did it without complaint. He moved her stuff and felt joy in his heart just to be near her in the privacy of her own home and away from the usual restrictions that work imposed. She even told him that he was pretty strong.

They talked a while. Then she opened a bottle of wine. They sat on the back porch in the furniture he'd just moved and cleaned, and they watched the people pass by in the alley below. A car with a broken muffler drowned out their speech and left a cloud of exhaust that lingered in the air. A squirrel on a telephone wire was suddenly running away from a crow that was dive-bombing it. In the upper air, seagulls drifting on the wind caught the evening light, notably orange against their wings, and beyond them were the clouds that Moore described to her.

Can you guess the type?

It's a cloud, she said.

It's an altostratus duplicatus, Moore said. Did you know that clouds have names?

I did not, she said.

I think clouds are the most beautiful things in the world, he said.

She laughed at that and said, I suppose you're one of those guys with your head stuck in the clouds.

Against a dead tree limb a woodpecker was hammering its beak. Moore took it all in and talked more compulsively than he should have. The subject of dinner came up. They went back and forth trying to decide—she didn't have a lot of money just yet for reasons she didn't want to go into. Moore said of course he'd pick up the tab. Money wasn't a problem. Finally they agreed on a restaurant.

Hold on a moment, let me change, she said.

Moore followed her into her apartment, the screen door slammed behind, and he sat in her living room waiting while she got dressed. He watched the evening sunlight cut orange bands of light into the darkening shadows of the room. Moore looked around hoping to understand something about her, but there wasn't much to look at. A run-down couch, an out-of-date TV, a nondescript picture on the wall, which was a satellite image of Earth with the words, in jubilant calligraphy: "The Blue Planet." Just then, Moore heard her call out: Hey, what are you doing over there? You don't have to wait out there. Come on over here.

She called him into the bathroom—Moore walked quickly, almost stealthily.

She was completely naked all of a sudden and applying makeup.

Sit, she said.

Moore sat.

Then she said, When I get stressed I like to relax by applying makeup.

Moore sat there on the tub looking at the beauty of her skin, the shape of her body, the sudden access to this private moment of hers and for a moment he was unable to say what he wanted to say because what he wanted to say was beyond saying. He was speechless. Dumbstruck. Struckdumb. Then he started talking again. He kept to the particulars. What do you think of this person at the office? he asked. What do you think of this and that person? How do you think our sales figures are going to turn out this year?

She listened to him carefully, and nodded. She said this person was okay, that one she didn't like too much. As to the numbers, that wasn't her concern.

How much longer do you think you're going to work here? he asked.

I don't know, she said.

Why are you thinking of moving on?

I haven't thought about it, she said. Oh wait, maybe I have. Sure, doesn't everybody think of moving on eventually? You don't want to get stuck working at a place like this forever, believe me.

Seriously? Moore asked. He had never heard of anyone talking like this about his company. It surprised him. He just assumed he'd grow old at a job like this.

Of course you also don't want to get stuck, she said. It's a boring job, really. And not really all that remunerative. This is a dead-end job, or a stepping-stone. For me it's the latter.

Moore became alarmed, sensing that she was bored with the work-related questions. So he just shut up and sat there speechless watching her apply her makeup. Against his will, he started twiddling his thumbs.

When she stepped away from the mirror she grabbed his hand and smiled.

You can deny the truth of what I just said, she said, but your eyes can't deny it.

What are you talking about?

You want to fuck me, she said. Not talk to me. I can tell.

That's not true, Moore said.

Most guys would have said the opposite, she pointed out. You, however, just won't say the truth of what you feel. But you don't need to. I can see that you like me.

Moore's heart sank.

I won't hold that against you. Do you still want to do dinner?

Yes.

135

Then why don't you stop babbling . . . Forget about eating earthly food and eat me instead.

She took his hand and led him to her bedroom.

Her bed, though a small twin, seemed capacious: a veritable kingdom tufted with pillows and an extravagant comforter, and though he should feel scrunched-in lying next to her, Moore felt as if he occupied a wide-open space. What was it Hamlet said? Moore tried to recollect . . . I could be bounded in a nutshell and consider myself a king of infinite space were it not that I have bad dreams? But this was not a bad dream. It was just the opposite. He was having sex with an apparition and so unlike Hamlet who was bound in his nutshell, Moore, under the sunny dream of Leanne, was the king, or rather a prince of endless space.

That was the joy of this, Moore thought, while she lies backside on the bed, his head crushed between her legs: it opens the mind. Another moment he thought: this is such a diversion from daily life where we can look but not touch, where we can think but not say. Here in this bed we are liberated to speak what we think, to do what we desire: to hold in our hands that which is real. This was a drug, Moore thought, and under the spell of it words were untethered from the great weight of duty that they were always tasked with: freighting meaning about to accomplish one thing or another. But it seemed like words were never let loose to say the unsayable: to speak the dream. But here, in her small bed, Moore began dreaming in the lightest language he could dream: this wasn't a bed but a great green lawn stretching to the horizon. On the lawn were scattered daisies and daffodils. It had been a wet spring. Magnolias were bursting the pod. Lilacs were on the bloom. There was jasmine in the air. Everything was green green and more green and the blue sky above wore a thin transparent veil of wispy cloud.

Moore heard her sigh. He had made her sigh! There were kites in the sky. Red-winged blackbirds twirred and twittered. A song was coming through her window—was it a flute or someone playing a desolate melody on a panpipe? Impossible to say, Moore muttered. Impossible to say. Moore kept saying the impossibility of saying: Impossible to say. Impossible to say. Impossible to say. Impossible to . . . until there was no more need for the saying and when they were done making love Moore rolled over and a moment later she dropped off to sleep.

She was completely knocked out like a narcoleptic, or was she dead? No, she was still breathing. Moore listened carefully, trying to decipher meaning from her breathing. Was it an elated breath or a spent breath? Moore lay down next to her—his brain thrumming. He wanted to do it again, right now. But she was unconscious from sleep. He lay next to her wondering what all this meant. She lay dead asleep apparently at ease with what it meant. He always had to try to fit it all together. Did she imply she was leaving the company? Did she really pass out or was she faking sleep? Was this a goodbye or was she staying and somehow declaring her love for him by falling asleep like this?

Why had she picked me? That was the most difficult point for Moore to understand. Sure, he had desired her, but he had never once expressed this desire. Maybe all she wanted was to talk. Maybe all she needed was a personal helper and for him to move a few things. Maybe all along she had just wanted him to install her air conditioning. Moore didn't know if she had a boyfriend. He assumed he didn't, but he could have been wrong. *Maybe she had never intended this. Maybe she grew impatient with the way I was looking at her. Maybe she just capitulated and gave up against the ferocity of my desire. I'll never know, will I?*

Moore lay awake until early morning waiting for her to open her eyes, and then he fell through a veil of dreams into the dark blank fathoms of sleep.

In the morning when she stirred, Moore woke immediately and came to life, but she took her shirt, which lay near her bed, put it on, and walked to the bathroom. She took a shower. He lay there

137

a moment savoring a peace that had settled over him, and then, remembering Rosemary—what would she think if she found out?—he felt a bit of regret and decided to get dressed.

When Leanne appeared again, her hair was wet and combed; she wore a sleeveless black top and a marvelous skirt that showed her legs. Moore realized then in a flash, belatedly, that not only did he have a crush on her but nothing would ever come of his crush. She smiled at him and said, Well, that was something.

Yes.

You'll have to go, though, she said. Someone, a friend, is coming to visit at eight thirty a.m. He went over to kiss her; she turned her head away and politely led him to the door.

Thank you, he said.

For what? she asked.

Of course, he said. For what?

Moore departed in a stupor and slept the whole day. He called her that evening to see how she was. He had waited because he wanted to give her (and himself) time to savor what had just happened. When she picked up the phone she explained that she couldn't talk because she was going to the movies with friends.

He called again late that night but she didn't answer. The following day he hoped to run into her at work but when he checked her schedule he saw that she was sent off to Arkansas for the first part of the week, and Texas for the second part of the week. He knew from conversations with her that next weekend she was leaving for two weeks to vacation in Puerto Rico. He tried desperately to get hold of her before she departed, but he failed.

When she returned to the office after a three-week hiatus he was gone on a weeklong sales call and he kept missing her. He assumed that since he wasn't getting her calls he was merely missing them. He kept checking his cell phone, his email accounts, all of them, and he even rather absurdly checked the hotel phone where he was staying—having the concierge ring his room—to make sure it worked. When he finally returned to the Chicago home office, he went to check her schedule and discovered that she was no longer with the firm. He drove to her apartment but she had moved out. No forwarding address was left. Who she was, where had she gone to, what did she do with the rest of her life, Moore never knew.

chapter 28
altostratus opacus

It was around this time that Rosemary inquired if he had had an affair.

What? Moore asked.

You know what, she said. Have you been with someone else?

Why do you ask?

Because I can tell something is up. You seem preoccupied. I talk to you but you don't listen to what I'm saying. The other night when I was telling you about my day, you fell asleep on me. Shame on you.

I was tired, Moore said.

Not interested is more like it. Just tell me the truth, did you have an affair?

There is no truth to tell, Moore said.

Oh yes, there is a truth to tell, Rosemary said. Only you're not telling it.

What is it with the women in my life always telling me I'm not telling the truth of what I think and feel? I would tell it but there's nothing to tell.

Fine. But let me say this, Jim, Rosemary said. If you tell me the truth now, we can work through it. If you want to remain mute like you remain mute on so many things, then we'll just call this the end.

I have nothing to say, Moore said.

Of course you don't, Jim. You never do.

And then she walked away: My back hurts. I need rest. Can you leave me be?

All right, Moore said, but I'll be back later.

That's fine. Come back in the morning. I'll have your things packed. Now goodbye.

Moore went back to his own apartment and instead of feeling remorse for what just happened with Rosemary, his brain went back to that evening he had with Leanne. *Why did she tantalize me with just one evening and then leave me without explanation? Why won't she call me back? Doesn't she want the happiness that we experienced that evening to go forward?* Moore thought of her leaning over her sink naked while he sat on the tub watching her. It was a gift. That's what he would say of it. She had given me the gift of a perfect evening.

Once the stabbing pain of Leanne's absence subsided (it had masked the greater loss of Rosemary), Moore tried to assess that greater more profound relationship. It seemed impossible to believe, in retrospect, that he had given up Rosemary for Leanne—and Moore couldn't even say who Leanne was—whereas the memories that filled his head surrounding Rosemary only seemed, with time, to abound more fruitfully.

For instance, Rosemary liked to play cards with him—straight poker. No one had ever played cards with him, though once, on a business trip, clients of Moore's had taken him to a casino riverboat, and it was aboard the smoky boat, crowded with gamblers, when Moore wandered over to the poker table. Moore played a few good hands that night and won unexpected large amounts, but the real prize came when, after his cards had been dealt to him, he had a flashback to sitting with Rosemary in her kitchen on a hot night, the windows open to the city, and there the two of them sat in perfect fellowship while Rosemary dealt the cards and Moore lifted them carefully from the card table to see what she had dealt him.

Rosemary was a marvelous person, Moore concluded that night so many years later at the riverboat casino. She was a gifted shuffler of cards, and an expert dealer, and she often dealt Moore the exact cards he needed. In retrospect, Moore could see that she knew the game well enough to know what he had and to give him what he needed and so she dealt him according to the tricks of a skilled shuffler those cards. It was a subliminal message that she was sending and it said this: I will help you get in life what you seek.

But it was so subliminal a message that Moore didn't realize until several years later that she had been communicating to him in this way and when he realized it on that riverboat, it was too late, of course. There was Leanne who had gotten between them and all the water of his various silences under the bridge.

Moore thinks of it now. Returning the next morning to Rosemary's apartment. His bags and all of his things were packed neatly for him at the door. Rosemary was such a completist. She packed his stuff so beautifully. He lifted the brass knocker on her door and before he could let it drop, she opened it for him and let him in. Her eyes were red-rimmed as if she had spent the night crying, or more probably, as if she hadn't gotten any sleep or both.

Moore stood before her. She was filled with suppressed emotion. He could tell she was afraid to say a word, lest one word unleash an unforgettable torrent that she would one day regret. She was holding herself firm against regret, against him. He thought to say something to her. Offer some explanation. Okay, it was a one-night stand. But her dignity threw him off this track. Instead, Moore decided to try to match her dignity. It was the least he could do. It was what the relationship required. The right ending here would send it off into

142

memory on the right footing. *One false move and all of this that we felt between us will be gone forever.*

Hello, Moore said. He looked directly into her eyes. He didn't attempt a smile.

Hi, Jim. I packed your bags. This should be everything.

You didn't have to.

I did.

Thank you.

For what? Rosemary asked him. She held her hands out. Palms up and empty. For what? Tell me, for what, Jim?

Moore put the palms of his hands down on hers without grasping her hands. They stood there with their hands touching like this for what seemed to him a remarkable period of time. Maybe two minutes. All the while they stared silently into each other's eyes. As Moore looked into her eyes he realized he had made a terrible mistake. It was a horrendous miscalculation. Rosemary had been the woman he had been looking for all along. She was his home, as she herself had so presciently stated. But now it was too late. She had given of herself freely and with incredible generosity, and now, because he had been selfish, because he had not been able to reciprocate her love, because he was so damned slow to understand, because, frankly, he was an idiot, it was over. *Shame on me,* he thought. *I deserve the treatment that comes my way.*

Just then she leaned over and gave Moore an ever so slight kiss on the lips and said, Goodbye, Jim.

Goodbye, Moore said, moderating himself to her lexical briefness and keeping his eyes steadily on hers.

Not removing his gaze, he reached down, grabbed all of his stuff that he had brought to her house in two hands. He smiled at last and said, You were good, Rosemary. You were the best. I won't forget you all the rest of my days. Thank you.

With that, Moore turned and walked down the hallway. When he turned left down the hall he heard Rosemary's door close.

And that was the last of her he had ever known for certain. The rest has resided only in his memory and imagination and in his darkest hours Moore can't discern one from the other.

chapter 29
altostratus pannus

Okay, the stately woman standing next to him said. Moore could tell she was a coach of some sort or another. Maybe she was a trainer. Moore opened his eyes and peeked at everyone scattered around the gate. No one seemed to notice him or care about what the two of them were doing. *For all they know, she and I are lifelong partners going through our stretches for the day.*

One last time, she said. Hands on hips.

Hands on hips.

Hands up in the air.

Up in the air.

Deep breath.

Okay.

Now bring your arms down.

Coming down.

Slowly.

Okay.

Your head; touch it.

Touching.

You are touching home. Completing a circle. Now back down to starting position.

He went to starting position.

Now squat. Deep breath. Pause. Okay, stand.

When he stood up, she turned and smiled at him. They were smiling at each other.

You're a quick learner, she said. Her voice was pleasant. Complimentary.

Thank you.

I can also tell you're easily preoccupied.

Yes, he said. All this waiting and now the yoga. It zones me out.

What are you zoning to, if you don't mind me asking?

He didn't mind her asking at all. It was a free world. Go ahead ask away.

Well, what?

Well, he said. Unlike you and your method, I try to keep a blank mind when I meditate. So I was thinking of nothing at all.

I'm a consultant, she said. A cursed job. Ten years ago when I took this job I thought it would be great to travel, see the world. In ten years I've only seen the inside of hotel rooms, stinky conference rooms, and airport terminals where I've wasted more than my share of life. How does one live a life so long in aircraft terminals?

I agree, Moore said.

You agree? How so?

I'm a sales rep with a too-vast territory or maybe just a half-vast territory.

You're a half-vast salesman!

She smiled and he smiled.

Yes, I'm a salesman or maybe just an ass. What did you think I am? Moore asked.

I don't know. You're dressed like a surgeon or something with those comfort shoes surgeons tend to wear, and the Adidas jacket. I saw you sitting there and couldn't figure out why no one would sit next to you. And then I thought, why not? He seems like a nice guy. People just must be intimated by him. What do you think?

I don't know, Moore said. I wake every morning and examine my face in the mirror and I see nothing to disturb the soul other than I'm getting older. Where are you headed?

Chicago, for one, and then down to Memphis.

Business? Moore asked.

We have a shop in Memphis, but I'm not headed down there for business. I'm renting a car in Chicago and then me and a couple of girlfriends are headed on a pilgrimage down I-57.

And you are headed where? Mecca or Memphis?

Elvis Presley. Graceland, is more like it. But yes, we will be staying in Memphis as well. Have you ever taken a pilgrimage? she asked.

I've never been to Graceland if that's what you mean?

But have you ever traveled anywhere just for the hell of it? Not to see the mountains or anything, but to visit some crazy place like Graceland?

I've been on one pilgrimage that I can think of. The Grand Canyon. Otherwise, no. I don't think I've ever been on a pilgrimage.

Everyone goes to the Grand Canyon, she said. That's not a pilgrimage. That's a rite of passage. Part of what it means to be an American. I'm talking about going on a trip for the sake of nothing.

Then no. I don't think I've ever been on a pilgrimage. Unless you want to call all the useless places in the middle of nowhere that I've been to for my work a pilgrimage. I've seen years and years of nothing.

What's funny? Me. I don't even like Elvis Presley but I'm going to see where he is buried anyway.

I like Elvis, Moore said. I mean some of it. I like the stuff he did on the Sun Sessions. But a lot of the other stuff I can do without.

What are the Sun Sessions?

The songs Elvis recorded at Sun Records, like "Blue Moon of Kentucky," "That's All Right (Mama)," "Mystery Train" . . . I used to sit and play cards with a friend in her kitchen on a hot summer night, the back door open to the sounds of the city, and we liked to play Elvis Presley songs. So they remind me of happy times.

Like I say, the Yogaist said. I don't even like Elvis.

I'd sing for you, Moore said, but I'm afraid it wouldn't come out right.

Good, she said. I hate public displays of singing. Karaoke drives me nuts. Do you like karaoke?

No, Moore said. Though I can't say I have much experience with it.

What's fun for the singer isn't necessarily fun for the rest of the audience who has to endure it.

It gets you drinking, I suppose, Moore said.

I suppose.

If you don't like Elvis, Moore asked, then why are you going to Graceland?

Her deep brown eyes turned to his.

Like I say, it's a pilgrimage. My girlfriends and I are going for fun. Something to do. A piece of nonsense. Graceland seemed like the perfect nonsensical place to go. Who knows what it'll be like? I might even find I like Elvis or that he's still alive.

He was something else.

Yes.

My mother collected all things Elvis.

Hmph. That's funny.

For Mom it wasn't funny. She loved everything Elvis ever sang. Even all those awful Hollywood B-sides. She used to play those over and over. She loved the way Elvis danced. I remember the day he died.

You do? she said. I was hardly born.

Well, I was just a kid when he died. When did he die? Just after Ford pardoned Nixon or something? Or was it later than that? My mom. It nearly killed her. She thought the Colonel had something to do with Elvis's death, and Mom was upset he was never charged.

With what? the Yogaist asked. Didn't Elvis overdose on drugs?

148

With negligence maybe, Moore said. Mom thought that the Colonel was a poor steward of Elvis's talent.

Your mom sounds like a pistol.

Thankfully, she had her quilt memorabilia to fall back on. And of course, Elvis's death only drove up the value of everything she owned.

Oh, the Yogaist said. Another reason why I'm going to Graceland . . .

Tell me.

Because my girlfriend got it in her head to do this trip. She's planning the whole thing. She teaches high school English where they make her teach *Beowulf* and Chaucer. She says Chaucer is all about a pilgrimage and so she wants to do one herself. There are all sorts of people taking pilgrimages these days. You could read about it on the internet if you want.

Moore smiled at her. Then he looked out the terminal at the snow falling; it was still falling down furiously.

Would you like to try another yoga position? she asked.

Do I have to?

Of course you do. As long as we wait here we may as well make the most of our time together, don't you think?

I don't think.

You can even call it part of my pilgrimage. By the way, I have a journal and you should be forewarned. Everything you tell me may end up in my journal.

Have I told you anything? Moore asked. I don't recall.

Yes. You told me your mother was a quilter. That's pretty neat, don't you think?

I would, I suppose, if she weren't my mom. But she's my mom. What can I say? We called her Sweet. And she was, sweet.

Where did you grow up? the Yogaist asked.

Iowa.

Wow. That's an incredible place.

Have you been there? Moore asked.

No, the woman said. I've flown over it. But I've always wanted to go there and see all the farms. Then out of the blue she said the word "Davenport."

It's nothing to look at, believe you me, Moore said.

Now there's where I disagree with you, the Yogaist said. Every place is a place to look at. It's the only attitude that has allowed me to survive so long in my business.

What shall we do next, great Yogaist? Moore asked.

May I recommend we bring metta into your life?

Metta?

It translates loosely as "loving-kindness."

Then by all means, yes.

Here's how you do it, the Yogaist said. Let me pull out a mat. You can do it with me on my mat. Okay, here . . .

You travel with a yoga mat?

Yes. It's essential for my sanity. Now first you sit on your duff. Right here on the mat next to me. Go ahead.

I'm on my duff.

No. Get down here on the mat next to me. Like this and on your duff.

Okay.

We're going to try a very simple asana. Do you know what an asana is?

No.

It's a yoga position. We'll start with something simple that I think you might like. It'll get your blood flowing a little bit, which is a good thing. You get so bottled up sitting in an airport like this. The blood just curdles around the ankles, don't you think?

I'll say, Moore said.

So here's how. First take off your Crocs. It's good you've got loose-fitting clothes.

I do it to pass quickly through security.

Smart. Now sit with your back straight and touch the bottoms of your feet together.

I'm too old for this.

Give it a try anyway. No need worrying about being perfect. It's good enough to be good enough. We can work toward perfection without worrying about achieving it.

Sounds like a good plan.

Okay. Now first. This may sound strange but please just go along with me a moment if you will. I'm only trying to help.

I'm going along, Moore said. I'm putty in your hands. Wood putty perhaps, but putty nonetheless.

We must learn to hold ourselves in the embrace of loving aware-ness. That's ultimately what yoga is all about.

It seems so threatening, all of this stretching.

It's liberating, really. Trust me.

I see.

We have to set ourselves up in a receptive, nurturing posture. Do you think you're ready for something like this?

For what?

For setting yourself up into a receptive, nurturing posture?

Time will tell.

My favorite position to start is the bound angle pose.

Ouch! I already hurt just thinking about it.

It's not that bad, believe me, the Yogaist said. But we may need a little space so don't be afraid. Ultimately, all that's required is that you do a gentle backbend.

Okay.

Now what I want you to do is try to hold yourself.

Now I've got to hold myself?

Hold yourself. Try to hold yourself in an embrace of loving aware-ness. Do you know what I mean? Go ahead, close your eyes and take notice, without judgment, of the emotional weather in your heart and the precise physical sensations that accompany it.

My heart feels like a clenched fist that's just gone fifteen rounds battering my opponent's granite jaw.

Then we must unwrap the bandages that bind your heart. Take hold of the bandages and tenderly start to peel them away, not pulling too quickly but not going too slowly either. Unwrapping the hurt and letting the heart breathe. I want you to go to a place where the fist of your heart opens up into a hand that . . . *gives*. Open the fingers of your heart one at a time. You have just gone fifteen rounds. I've taken the gloves off your hands. We have slowly unwrapped the bandages. Breathe in. Breathe out. I'm cutting the tape. Your hand-heart is bruised, but it's filled with love. Unclench what the hand holds and release the love it contains.

This is better than air travel, Moore said, trying to unclench his metaphysical heart-hand.

You're cute, she said.

Thank you. You're the first person to tell me that in years.

I don't believe it's been that long for a guy like you.

Are you trying to make emotional weather in my heart or focus my attention on it?

A little of both, maybe. Now. Do you find this mat comfortable?

Comfortable enough.

Good, the Yogaist said. Now get down like this with your legs and arch your back gently, watch me. There you go. I see that you're actually trying. Very impressive!

In wrestling we called this the bridge.

You're good at it. Not to mention, you're flexible.

I'm a quick learner is more like it, Moore said.

Okay, now let's focus this intention. You can do so by uttering these metta phrases. Repeat after me, will you?

I will.

Then say, May I be peaceful and joyful.

May I be peaceful and joyful.

May my body be well.

May my body be well.

Breathe with me and say it again, synchronizing your breath to the phrases.

Say, May I be peaceful and joyful.

May I be peaceful and joyful.

May my body be well.
May my body be well.
May my clenched fist open itself.
Clenched fist open.
May it release giving love.
Giving love.

Now hold it there and focus your attention on the physical. Can you feel your aching hip joints? Can you feel the pulse in your throbbing knees? Understand the burn around your exhausted eyes, and the fatigue of your tired brain. Now slowly let yourself go into a space of ease and well-being. *You are a bird. Remember? A red-winged blackbird. We are in a grassy meadow on the edge of the forest. The breeze is gentle, cool, and filled with the smell of clover . . .*

chapter 30
altostratus praecipitatio

Moore was sixteen years old. He had just learned how to drive and as a reward his parents decided that he would be the primary driver on their road trip. They had taken a car trip from Iowa. He drove the whole way: Newton, Iowa, to Sedona, Arizona: a total of fourteen hundred miles. Moore had had his license less than a week.

Moore's father was anxious that they get there without stopping for a motel because he didn't want to spend money on the motel. It wasn't that his father was cheap, only that he never had a lot of money. They lived a hand-to-mouth existence. What's more, the vacation was planned on a whim, and thus his father had tapped their bank account of what little reserves he had managed to save up the past few years. It wasn't much, but a vacation was overdue and the kid needed practice driving.

Moore was allowed to give up the wheel anytime he pleased, but if he wanted to, he could drive as far as he wanted. I'll chase the sun, Moore thought, as it falls over the western rim.

His father sat at his side, his mother in the back seat. It had always been his father in the driver's seat, his mother in the passenger seat, and he always rode in the back. But now he displaced his father, and his father displaced his mother, who had taken the position of the child in the back seat. His father had never been voluble. He spent most of the trip with his elbow hanging out the window, staring at the fields of corn, which gave way to wheat and pasture and sand hills and the high plateau of the Great Plains, and then mountains.

His father, when he talked, spoke of the land. Look at those fields, he would say. Or, That's an awful lot of corn that farmer planted. It ain't nearly as tall as ours back home, but they don't have the rain we do. Or he'd speak of cloud types that formed in the open skies as the day heated up and clouds massed on the horizon. A lot of altostratus praecipitatio this afternoon, look out that-a-way to the northwest . . . see it? Often enough, his father just liked to express the simple awe he felt looking at the clouds. Look at them clouds over there, he would say, while Moore was driving, his eyes fixed on the road ahead. Aren't those clouds just beautiful? Like a floating mountain range. And the things they tell you about the weather. Over the years, I've learned how to read the sky like an open book just by looking at the clouds. White clouds. Blue skies and the green of the cropland. It makes for a perfect day.

Moore guessed that his father spoke in a normal voice to keep everything calm in the car while Moore drove, both hands on the wheel, in the left lane passing trucks. Moore was certain his mother sat in the back seat in a quiet state of unrelieved panic. His father had asked him: how does the car handle? It was an honest question from one man to another. Moore took a moment to answer, and in measured tones he had said: Drives nice, Dad.

It's a good car.

Yes.

Pontiac makes a good car. It sure is a hell of a sight better than that old Ford that blew up on us, remember?

Moore doesn't know why this memory comes to him all of a sudden while he's doing yoga in the airport, but it's a memory of his parents and as such it's valuable. He had never before thought about this trip.

Not long into the journey, his father had asked him if he wanted to change drivers, to take a break.

No, Moore said.

Suit yourself.

Moore was afraid that if he yielded the driver's seat he wouldn't get it back. He was also afraid that he would appear weak. He wanted so much to be strong, unbreakable, like his dad. He wasn't about to break down and hand over the wheel, so he drove at first with joy stinging his heart nearly eighty miles an hour down the highway heading to Wichita, Kansas, a place he had always heard about but never seen, much less visited. A massive anvil cloud was on the horizon and they were driving directly toward it. His father, watching the cloud as they got closer, confirmed what he saw. It's a cumulonimbus incus cloud, Jim, his father said. We're in for some rough weather.

It was storming with hail and slashing rain and high winds when they hit Wichita, and Moore pulled under a viaduct until the worst of the storm abated. Moore remembers the car getting buffeted by wind even as they sat under the viaduct for shelter and his mother chattered on and on in the back seat about every tornado she had lived through living out on the open plains.

And it wasn't like *The Wizard of Oz*, she said at some point. It was worse.

It's always worse to live through them, his father said.

When the storm cleared, Moore pulled out from under the viaduct and kept on driving for hours on end on US-54 with increasing fatigue and concern as the journey stretched on through the endless barren spaces of the Southwest. He realized without admitting it that all he wanted to do was take a nap and get some sleep.

Moore remembers pulling off at a rest stop where they all got some sleep, and then his father took over the wheel while it was still deep night, and he proceeded to drive the rest of the trip, where they spent the week in a tent alongside Oak Creek, fishing, swimming, and just swinging in the hammock. But Moore had been right. Once he relinquished the wheel, he never got it back.

Prior to this moment, that trip west with his parents had all but been lost in the past, but now here, doing yoga with the Yogaist—bent backward in what position did she call it—bound angle pose?—it had come rushing back into him as if dislodged or jettisoned from some junkyard of memory. Before Moore could think another thought about it the Yogaist said:

Now get up and sit down, if you can.

It was her voice bringing him back.

Hello, she said. Are you okay? Do you think you can get out of your position?

I was meditating, Moore said.

I see that.

And I had a new memory of a road trip I took once long ago with my parents. It too was a sort of pilgrimage or rite of passage, I suppose. Thank you. Prior to today, I had completely forgotten that trip.

You're welcome, she said. I'm happy to help.

Moore tried to release himself from bound angle pose, but he felt stuck. Glued in place. His thigh muscles were burning as if shredded.

He tried to budge from his position but couldn't. I need help, he said. I've been twisted into a pretzel and I can't undo myself. Please, help.

She reached over and gently supported Moore as he moved out of his position. Her hold was firm and filled with care. He undid himself, then stood up, stretched a bit as if returning from a deep slumber, and slipped his Crocs back on his feet. The floor was unspeakably filthy and his socks must now be contaminated. The Yogaist turned and looked at him. Moore smiled at her.

Listen, she said. Do you mind doing me a huge favor?
Anything.

Can you watch my bags? I need to go to the bathroom. It's been hours since I . . .

157

Go. Go. Please, go. I'll watch your bag. Of course.

I'll be right back, she said.

You better be right back or I'll be arrested for harboring the bag of a stranger!

Thanks.

With that she was off, across the concourse toward the bathroom, and instead of dodging into the toilet, she just kept walking until she was out of sight. She had a funny walk, Moore thought. He had seen nothing like it, exactly. It made him nervous to see her walk away and sooner than he thought, she disappeared.

chapter 31
altostratus radiatus

Moore looked across the gate at all the people. Had they noticed him? Most were asleep. Those that were awake looked bored out of their wits and couldn't care less what happened just as long as the airplane showed up soon.

Moore thought about his behavior. *I'm a perfectly regular citizen*, he thought, *but if a woman shows up—particularly an attractive one—I'm always going out on a limb to please her. It's small-minded of me and ridiculous to be so deferential to a potential sex partner.*

Moore thought back to his days in Iowa and how they collected stray dogs. They attached a female in heat to the back of a truck and drove slowly through town. All afternoon the stray male dogs would come from backyards and open fields, from the woods and the cemeteries, attracted by the female and one by one they'd be impounded. *That's the kind of dog I am. I'm someone who would get caught in such a simple trap.*

It embarrassed Moore to think he was hardly different than a horny dog. But it was more than that, more than sex, wasn't it? *I want a partner, someone to talk to and argue with.* Once he had someone, then he could get on with pursuing all the great things he had put off.

He wished he could think beyond such grim necessity as finding a partner. *It's the thing that stops me from doing other things of greater merit.*

Moore thought of the great poem by Dylan Thomas . . .

He had memorized it while he was still a student at college. Yes, he remembers it now. *That's one memory resurrected from the past—that I used to memorize poems!* His favorite poem was Dylan Thomas's "And Death Shall Have No Dominion." Moore could still quote a portion of it by heart:

Twisting on racks when sinews give way,
Strapped to a wheel, yet they shall not break;
And the unicorn evils run them through;
Split all ends up they shan't crack;
And death shall have no dominion.

Moore still liked the poem: the rising energy of it, the call it made; its refusal to yield. It spoke to those heroic souls who naturally wanted what they couldn't have—immortality—but they sought vaingloriously to obtain it anyway. The most ardent among them scaled their so-called summits untethered or flew, like Icarus, too close to the sun. But they often died in cruel and violent ways. And unlike Icarus, no one cared to remember them. Nevertheless, nice as Dylan Thomas's sentiment was in the poem, it didn't make sense, really, for death always wins out. It had dominion over everything: dominion over weak, dominion over strong; dominion over everything in between. There was no way around this truth, Moore thought, because immortality is but a dream cast by poets.

But Dylan Thomas was a fabulous poet! How he could put the word to something. Once when Moore was in Greenwich Village, he went to the White Horse Tavern to pay his respects. It was one of Dylan Thomas's last watering holes. Moore remembers the night. He wandered around Lower Manhattan and the Village all night in the rain stopping under awnings from time to time to keep dry, looking for the White Horse Tavern, and when he finally found it, it was twenty minutes until closing time.

Moore opened the door, stepped into the bar, and there was a lovely gleaming quality about the place. He sat down on a stool, ordered a beer. He looked around the place; there was the head of a white horse above the bar—was it plasticine or plastic . . . who could tell? In a voice barely audible, Moore quoted a fragment or two from Dylan Thomas's poetry:

Do not go gentle into that good night.
Rage, rage against the dying of the light.

Dylan Thomas, the bartender said, overhearing Moore, who was still wet from the rain.

Yes!

We hear his lines around here from time to time. That line is the most famous.

It means something, I suppose.

Yeah, the bartender joked. The rage I get when I turn on the lights at the end of the night and make the last call. That's what it means to me.

They both laughed at the bartender's joke.

It was good to know a poem or two, Moore thought. It was nice also to pay homage to the dead who had become our friends in a way, because their words had become part of our lives. That's the gist of what he told the bartender. He was proselytizing but it wasn't for naught because he was drinking Laphroaig 10. The bartender let him drink a few extra on the house after closing time and then shooed him out at three a.m.

I suppose my Yogaist would be impressed with these lines. At some point, maybe we will even talk about it.

Do you like poetry? she might ask him (and how thrilling to be asked, he'd never been asked this question before).

Yes, as a matter of fact, Moore would say, I love poetry and this is my favorite poem, a thing by Dylan Thomas.

I like poetry too, the Yogaist might say.

What kind of poetry do you like?

Well for one, I like all the songs of Joni Mitchell and if you study the lyrics closely you'll see they are every bit poems.

Yes.

What do you like?

Dylan Thomas.

Oh, I've heard of him.

Do you know any of his poetry?

No, do you?

As a matter of fact, I do. At which point Moore would quote the poem. He loved to say it full-throated. Afterward he might even tell the Yogaist that Dylan Thomas was an alcoholic. He wrote, among other things, *Under Milk Wood*.

Never heard of it, she might say.

I'll read it to you one day. You'll like it. I read it every year right around Christmastime, which is a good time for that piece.

Wow. You really know a lot about him!

As I'm sure you know a lot about Joni Mitchell!

Outside the White Horse Tavern, the rain had stopped. Moore hailed a cab and was back at his Midtown hotel. In the lobby, a woman was lounging on a chair. Moore was feeling drunk enough from his night out and all the free shots of whiskey from the bartender that, on a whim, he offered for the woman to come up with him to his hotel room.

To Moore's surprise the woman took him up on his offer. In the elevator going up to his room, he happened to notice that her incisors both upper and lower were missing, as if they had been pulled. It was disconcerting to say the least, but even more disconcerting was the fact that not only did Moore not care, but he found her dimpled smile charming, alluring. What was the word he had been looking for: it was a mirthful, Giaconda smile. What else could it be with

162

those essential teeth missing? A tiger without a bite? A defanged snake in the Garden of Eden? When the shark bites, with her teeth, dear . . . No, this song wouldn't apply to her.

Nevertheless, Moore smiled back at her, then closed his mouth. He didn't feel it was polite to show off his own perfectly aligned and whitened teeth. What's more, he was unexpectedly drunk, and under such conditions, he didn't trust himself.

When they entered Moore's room, the woman wrapped her arms around him, then took off her clothes. Moore put his tongue in her mouth just to feel with it the holes where her incisors had been. A moment later he removed his clothes and they were having sex. He was astonished at the speed that things were moving.

A moment later she was in the bathroom. He heard her make a couple of odd grunting or coughing sounds, the toilet flushed. She returned to the room, standing in front of him, back in her clothes.

That will be seventy-five dollars, she said.

It took Moore by complete surprise.

You're joking, he said.

He had no idea she was a prostitute. Weren't terms supposed to be discussed in situations like this? Instead, she came on to him as if she liked him.

No. I am not joking. Don't make me call security. Seventy-five dollars, she said again. This time her voice had a surprising edge to it. Moore reached for his wallet. All he had was eighty. She stood over him as he counted it, otherwise he would have offered sixty.

Here, Moore said, handing over the money. He was confused. He was frightened of the security she had just mentioned. He felt vulnerable all of a sudden. He felt a stranger in a strange place.

She didn't say thank you, but she did pause a moment and look thoughtfully into his face. If you hadn't come inside me it would only have been sixty. But now I got to deal with what happens to me if you just made me pregnant.

You don't have protection? Moore asked.

No. Nor did you, daddy! With that, she was out the door and out

163

of his life. Moore couldn't believe it. The possible mother of his child had just stepped into and out of his life. He would never know.

Even though it was four thirty in the morning, Moore packed his bags immediately and, still a little drunk, he was off to the airport to catch a nine a.m. plane. The lady at the front desk was efficient and didn't say a word. But oddly, she smiled at him and told him: Have a nice afternoon.

On the flight home, and on countless flights home thereafter, Moore often found himself wondering if indeed he had made the woman pregnant. To think, he thought, all she asked of me was an additional twenty dollars. What was left was the memory of those missing teeth, his tongue moving around the sockets in her mouth where those teeth had been, and those odd grunting sounds she made on her own after they had had sex.

How long ago was that? Five, maybe six years ago? And now here he was waiting for the Yogaist to return. Moore thought of those dogs from his youth arriving from the four corners of town because they smelled something in the air. We all have our secrets, like those dogs, until they're brought out in the open and we're impounded.

Would I share this secret with anyone? Moore wondered. He hadn't so far, and he thought he probably never would. Better in cases like this to let bygones be bygones.

chapter 32
altostratus translucidus

Moore took a proprietary interest in the Yogaist. *I wonder if she has someone.* The word "stately" came back to mind. Across from Moore was the woman who had been chattering on the phone. She had laid her head back on the chair, closed her eyes, and fallen asleep. Her mouth sagged open. Her boy's head was on her lap; he was sleeping as well.

The gentleman reading the *Wall Street Journal* was also asleep, his paper crumpled in his lap, and his son, leaning against the man's shoulder, was playing a handheld digital game that made irritating noises. *No problem,* Moore thought. *I can handle irritating noises like that now that I have my Yogaist.*

Moore thought of the Yogaist—*What vitality she possesses! The nerve of her to come over to me and insist that I start doing yoga with her!* He was very impressed with her. He nearly said the words "loving-kindness" out loud.

The heavy man across from Moore was eating a large ice cream cone and drinking from an extra-large Coke. He returned Moore's stare. Moore didn't budge from looking at the man even as the man's head bobbed slightly to the straw and sucked up more Coke. *He had probably watched me perform yoga with my Yogaist.*

What was her name? Moore wondered. He was always forgetting to get the name. Her bag was next to his feet. He supposed he could lean over and check to see if there was some name tag associated with the bag, but on second thought, he would wait to ask her. It would be an invitation to talk.

Moore would ask her what her name was, and she in turn would inquire as to his name. He would tell her what his was, and then they might talk a little about work. What do you do? he would ask. She'd tell him, then she'd ask him about his work. They'd go from work, to where do you live, to what do you like to listen to, to zodiac, and favorite foods, and sports and so on and so forth and on the inquisitional questions would continue until the spark of more spontaneous conversation caught fire or the opposite took hold: silence.

Moore often feared silence in these early encounters. He thought empty space in early conversations was often too morbid and often led to the quick demise of budding possibility. He knew that it was all a matter of perspective. If he was talking to a woman who was more comfortable with silence than he, then early silence might not dampen so quickly the possibility of love, but invariably his own discomfort with conversational silence would leave him tongue-tied whether he liked it or not—and once that happened, he had to disengage, get a drink, stand up and walk around. Or twiddle his thumbs. But sitting there staring at his hands wondering how to respond to his interlocutor was too much to bear.

Moore kept looking over at the heavy man eating ice cream. *I wonder if he saw me doing yoga with my Yogaist. He must be thinking that I'm crazy. What was it she was showing me? Mountain pose?* Moore looked at his watch. He'd been sitting here for hours. *How long is it the Yogaist has been gone? She said she was just going to the bathroom.* Moore racked his brain trying to remember if she had said anything else. Did she say she was also getting something to eat? He tried to think if he had offended her in some way. *Was it something I said?* Impossible, because he had hardly said a word. Why had she come over to him in the first place? Maybe she was an opportunist. *She saw me sitting cross-legged and misinterpreted me. She thought I too was into yoga because of how I was sitting and she may have only wanted a yoga partner.*

However, I was only sitting like that to keep the blood flowing. Maybe she saw that I was trying to keep the blood flowing and saw it as an opportunity to introduce herself to me through yoga. Yet no sooner do we get introduced than she's off. I was just getting out of that bridge position when she excused herself for the bathroom and left.

Then there was that funny walk of hers and instead of turning in to the bathroom, she kept on walking down the concourse until she was out of view. It was strange and Moore wondered if he should take off after her. Go follow her. Find out who she is and what she's doing. Moore felt embarrassed all of a sudden to be in this fix. *I should just forget I ever met her, or better yet, I should be patient and wait for her to return. Wait long enough and the blizzard might die down and off we go toward home.*

I can sit and wait for her and the plane or I can stretch my legs with a walk and learn more. There was no time posted as of yet as to the departure of the plane. Any staff related to this flight had been gone from the check-in counter for at least the past hour. Where were they? They were probably sitting in some canteen somewhere with other airport workers. *For that matter, where is the priest? He was gone. All of that time staring at me and now he's gone and I didn't even notice him leave. So too is the old lady who had collapsed next to the priest on the verge of breathing her last. If they decided it was okay to get up and walk around, isn't it also okay for me to get up walk around a bit and also pass the time?*

The question arose what to do with his bag and hers. Moore was taking a proprietary interest in the Yogaist's property as if it already belonged to him. *How stupid can I be, falling for such a caper.* But on second thought Moore wondered if, in the scheme of things, it hurt to be protective of her bag. *Should I carry her bag and my bag with me and stake out after her?* And if he does manage to catch up with the Yogaist, then what? What happens next? First he would get unzippered. *Personal exposure,* Moore thought. *Questions of who I am and where I came from.* Excavations of his soul. What was it like, she would invariably ask him, growing up in Iowa?

It was unbearable to contemplate and it was only a matter of time before they got to these all-too-tedious questions.

chapter 33
altostratus undulatus

Moore remembered back to Rosemary. They went out one night on their first anniversary. Rosemary had arranged the evening. First they would go to a roadside carnival, then they'd go out to a Mexican cantina for food. The carnival was crowded and Rosemary immediately took Moore to the Zipper, her favorite ride. While they were waiting in line at the Zipper, a god-awful spin ride of centrifugal force seemingly designed to rip and twist out your guts, Rosemary had casually asked the question: So tell me, Jim, I don't mean to pry, but tell me what it was like growing up in Iowa? Unzip a little.

When Moore looked at her, he rolled his eyes. Please, you can ask any question. Just don't ask me what it was like growing up in Iowa.

But that night, for some reason, Rosemary didn't stop asking.

While they were on the Zipper, or more precisely, while he was being spun around so he felt his guts in his throat and felt on the verge of puking, Rosemary had had the temerity to ask in the blowing wind of the ride: Tell me, Jim Moore! Tell me now. Do or die. What was it like growing up on a small farm in Iowa?

They were being whipped around; Rosemary's long hair was flying in the air. If her back bothered her that night, she didn't let on, and just when he thought he could take the spinning ride no more he

169

said the honest truth: Die! I'd rather die, Rosemary, then talk about my childhood in Iowa. Please stop asking me these questions and please have them stop this crazy ride, I'm going to puke! As if the operator heard him, the ride slowed, and then came to a stop, and they were unlocked from the cagelike contraption and set free onto the carnival grounds.

Moore was too discombobulated to even stand. He thought he still might puke, so he found a bench and sat feeling more sick than he had felt in years. It reminded him of a childhood fever he had experienced, and the loneliness of being locked up in his room for days on end with the window open to the land and the big fluffy alto-stratus undulatus clouds rolling in from the horizon. Moore thought he might tell her of that memory, but he was too sick to speak. He was sick enough that he didn't even want to have dinner. Instead, he just begged off for the evening.

Let's go home, Moore said. I feel too sick to go another step.

You do look a little peaked, Rosemary said, and home they went and that was the last of it until she asked it again. What was it like growing up in the middle of nowhere? Tell me about flyover country . . .

Dig or pry and when there was nothing to excavate, Rosemary kept digging and prying. It became a problem.

What had started out promising enough, this relationship with Rosemary, ended up becoming all too real and trivial, always focused on his past, on Iowa, on what it was like growing up in that house. But there was nothing to report because his past was nothing and perhaps that's what ultimately drove them apart.

chapter 34
altostratus virga

The Yogaist seems promising to Moore. They all seem promising when you first meet them . . . when they are still absolute strangers. It was only when they began to dig and pry trying to get you to open up by asking questions about your childhood, when they and the relationship seemed all too real. At that point, Moore often wanted nothing more to do with it. But why was that? What would it have taken to share a simple memory of his childhood? For instance, what about this story . . . Moore had never told it, he had never even tried to put it into words, but somehow it always lingered in the mumble of his own internal hum waiting to be released into human speech. It was the story of waiting for his parents to come home from their vacation.

Moore couldn't tell this story because it was too hard to tell so he never told it. Instead he is always stuck at that moment.

He's sitting in the parlor of his grandparents' house that was located in town waiting for his folks to come home. There he is now. He can see it. He's sitting near the window looking out on the street from a gap in the drapery which is blowing gently in the breeze from the open window. A postal carrier walks up the steps and deposits the day's mail into his grandparents' postal box. He hears the mail fall into the box and the door of the box shut, and the postal carrier walking back down the steps of the sidewalk. A group of kids walk by idly bouncing a ball between themselves. A crow playing with a stick in its mouth as if it were a third limb turns a pop cap over near the curb in search of what? Occasionally a car drives by on the street, or a delivery truck carrying milk or bread or a workman's truck carrying tools and ladders.

In the distance there is a neon sign that mesmerizes Moore. It's in the shape of a hot dog and it advertises Murphy's Red Hots. He liked to go to Murphy's with his grandfather and pile the green piccalilli which itself was a neon shade of green on the red hot dog. He'd squirt mustard just to provide a countervailing shade on the green spectrum, and then he'd dose it up with ketchup for flavor and flair. The fries were good too. They were slender and long and curled as they popped and fizzled in the deep-fat fryer. They came served in a plain brown bag with liberal amounts of large-grain salt, and you would shake the fries just to make sure the salt distribution was adequately applied to each fry.

The sign itself was alluring—he knows now that the sign proba-bly dated back to the mid-1950s, but as a kid he only knew that the blinking round-bulbed lights, which flashed in synchronicity around the hot dog like a race car going endlessly around the track, signified something painfully cosmopolitan and wonderful and what's more, it tasted like hot dog.

And then as if the wait might never come to an end—what has become of his parents? Did they die in some brutal car accident? Had they decided to stay in New York, leaving him and his fate in the hands of his grandparents? But no, nothing at all happened to them. From around the corner, their white Ford Fairlane approached. His father pulled up into the driveway, and a moment later his mom car-rying a bag filled with packages, and his dad in a new hat, emerged from the car. They came up the steps and upon seeing Moore they embraced him in tears.

We missed you, Jim, darling.

172

How wonderful to see you, James! We promise not ever to leave you behind like this again.

Just wait until you see all the pictures we snapped of New York City!

How were Grandma and Grandpa? Did you have a restful time away from us? We love you, et cetera, et cetera.

That's what happened, which is to say, nothing happened. The clocks in his grandparents' house, for his grandfather had been a great collector of clocks, only ticked the passage of the afternoon in the quiet parlor just as he awaited the return of his parents. They would not record the agonizing fear he felt waiting for them; they would not record the boredom he felt waiting, the boredom, which almost seemed to push him outside the ken of time. Tick. Tock. Tick. On it would go until his parents would finally arrive on tick. Tock. The clock moving inexorably as the moment of their arrival approached, then arrived, and then drifted into the past taking everyone associated with that moment with it—his grandparents, his parents— receding into a past nearly beyond recovery into the blur of his internal hum and on the clock of time would tick until one day Moore suffered his own silent death of unknown causes. And what could those causes be but death by boredom, death by waiting, death by whiling the afternoon away in a place you didn't want to be in, powerless to alter the events and be somewhere else, doing anything else under the sun other than this waiting.

Was that afternoon any different than this air travel? In a way, Moore had been bred for this sort of existence: bred to be waiting, bred to be idle. And then there was the endless pain of coming up with an answer to the question: What was it like growing up in Iowa? or, How did your trip to Southern California go? How to say: nothing happened, it was completely uneventful—I waited and waited and waited?

In the springtime when I was a boy, I would lie in the grass in the front yard of our house. I'd lie on my back and I'd watch the clouds roll by for hours on end and I would try to name the clouds as my father had taught me. I could do that for hours on end. I could do it in the sunshine; I could do it in the snow. I wasn't even afraid of thunderstorms. I'd lie there in the mud watching the clouds fly overhead and I would try to name every cloud formation. That was my childhood. It was a childhood without incident or story, and even though I am unable to fill a moment telling you about my day or life, I am still happy I lived it. I am still happy to be living it. I am still happy. See, I told you there was nothing to report. It was all of a piece.

cumulus fractus, cumulus humilis, cumulus mediocris, cumulus congestus; stratocumulus castellanus, stratocumulus lenticularis, stratocumulus stratiformis; stratus fractus, stratus nebulosus, stratus opacus, stratus translucidus, stratus undulatus; cumulonimbus calvus, cumulonimbus capillatus, cumulonimbus incus, cumulonimbus mammatus, cumulonimbus pannus, cumulonimbus pileus, cumulonimbus praecipitatio, cumulonimbus spissatus, cumulonimbus velum, cumulonimbus tuba, cumulonimbus virga; altocumulus perlucidus; altostratus duplicatus; mammatus; altostratus nebulosus, altostratus opacus, altostratus pannus, altostratus praecipitatio, altostratus radiatus, altostratus translucidus, altostratus undulatus, altostratus virga; cirrostratus nebulosus; nimbostratus pannus, nimbostratus praecipitatio; cirrus castellanus; nimbostratus virga

chapter 35
cirrostratus nebulosus

Moore stood in the washroom taking a piss. Ahhhh . . . Thank goodness, he thought. The piss felt good. He held his in too long too often. He had a good bladder, but at what price to his kidneys? Sometimes Moore became irrational and worried about renal failure, at which point it didn't matter what part of the business deal he was in—hell, he could be closing a huge account—he'd interrupt and say, Do you mind? I need to step out for a moment.

This was such a moment.

Moore had left the Yogaist's bag next to his seat. To show solidarity, he also left his bag by hers. It seemed reasonable. No one would steal it. What would they do with his bag? There was nothing in it, except his papers and a week's worth of soiled clothes. What's more, they had all spent so much time together at the gate, it was as if everyone knew each other. *The heavy man alone will watch my bag. That's all he seems capable of doing: eating and watching me.*

The urinals lined the wall, and scattered down the row were a half-dozen guys staring at the wall in front of them. What a life. We're cattle, after all, Moore thought. We're all standing around pissing in a trough waiting for the final hammer blow to strike right between our eyes.

The guy pissing next to Moore whistled but what did he whistle? Was that "Dixie"? Did anyone nowadays really whistle "Dixie"? It seemed impossible to believe and yet there it was for his very own ears to hear! Another dude, two urinals away, mumbled under his breath limning the nether reaches of an unspeakable thought with the words, fucking-goddamned-fucking-goddamned-pussy-fuck . . .

One or two of the stalls were occupied and then there was a shit, a huge explosion of shit and gas—and the wet smattering sound of diarrhea followed by volumes of loose wet chunks that uncorked from the bowels of the traveler into the waters of the toilet bowl. From the adjacent stall ushered more human grunting as some soul tried to put in motion with one great bowelic push a digestive system that had stalled, seized up, all but stoppered by a huge, hard turd.

It was the plight of the inveterate traveler: a digestive system that never seemed to catch its rhythm. When it came time to shit you were always marooned in one of these all too public places trying to control the disgusting sound yet let go the necessary release. It was all so public and humiliating and Moore had never gotten used to it; he only pitied those who suffered a similar fate. Indeed, when the diarrhea guy stepped out of his stall, a bit dazed, the two of them exchanged sympathetic glances. *Yeah, I know what you just went through. Welcome to the brotherhood of the traveling salesman. Now move on, dark horseman, move on.*

As Moore stood taking a leak his stomach growled. He was hungry. Last time he ate was this morning. It was in his hotel room. He had room service deliver a croissant with butter wrapped in foil and a packet of grape jam. There was a pot of coffee. It arrived as he was stepping from the shower. Moore wrapped himself in the hotel robe, then let the valet into the room to deposit the continental breakfast on the desk in the bedroom. Moore tipped the valet a buck and without further ado, closing the door behind the valet, he went back to his desk, took a bite of the croissant, and sipped the coffee.

Moore parted the drapes on his window and looked out onto the highway that his room abutted. It was a gray and dismal day. Truck-

176

ers and early-morning rush-hour traffic were already stalling on the slushy and icy road. It was a Thursday. Snow pushed by high winds was falling out of the sky and it seemed to make a bad traffic situation worse. The view out Moore's window was miserable. Beyond the road was a mall, and beyond the mall was a hill with high-tension wires and cell phone towers competing for space with rows of neatly planted spruce trees. In a few moments he too would be out on that very highway contending with the elements and thus would begin his day and his long slog home.

Moore sat back down at the desk, which now served as a table, and ate his food. He tried to eat as carefully as possible. One of the problems about traveling alone was that should food become lodged in the trachea, there would be no one around to perform the Heimlich maneuver. It made Moore sad—as if he had failed some fundamental task in life—that he often found himself eating alone away from anyone who might perform the lifesaving move on him.

Moore had learned the Heimlich maneuver while a junior in high school. There's a childhood memory for you, Moore thought while eating his croissant. The Heimlich dummy sat on a chair at the front of his class in his science classroom. His teacher—he remembers him now, Mr. Hyde, though he was known to everyone in the school as Doctor Jekyll—had the dummy, Frankenstein, in the classroom, and there they lined up along the chalkboard, each classmate taking a turn trying to dislodge *by compression of the abdomen* just below the diaphragm a plastic food item that had been stuck in the dummy's throat. When it was Moore's turn, he wrapped his arms around the dummy and squeezed so hard that the piece of plastic food lodged in the dummy's throat shot out airborne, smacked high up on the opposite wall, and fell to the ground.

Well, Mr. Hyde said. I see that you are at least a good shot, Jim. Just don't try to squeeze so hard on a real human. You might break some ribs.

Moore zipped his pants and washed his hands at the tap. He sudsed both sides of his hands and washed above his wrists. He liked to wash himself like a surgeon. You can never be too careful with the germs in a place like this. While he washed his hands, he accidentally caught a view of himself in the mirror and once again he was shocked by what he saw.

Moore cupped his hands under the tap and brought the water to his face. Then he sudsed up under the soap dispenser with pink foam soap. He washed all around his neck and underneath his ears. He cupped his hands again under the water and started rinsing his face and neck, carefully trying not to get his collar wet. When Moore was done washing, he stood at the hand blower, tilted it up toward his face, and let the hot air blow on his head. In the torrent of noise and wind, Moore forgot, for a moment, who he was.

chapter 36
nimbostratus pannus

As Moore stepped out of the men's room, he bumped into three guys coming into the bathroom, and as he entered the concourse he saw yet more men headed this way. It was too many hours in the airport, and now the great crowd of humanity was migrating to empty their discharge into the flushing toilets.

It felt good to walk and stretch his legs. Moore walked alongside the automatic walkway—and a couple of kids were playing on it, but Pimp Boy had apparently moved on. There was a Houlihan's canteen and a crowd was gathered around the bar drinking. The television sets were broadcasting NBA basketball games. Moore had half a mind to duck in for a beer, but he also had half a mind to wander around the airport looking for the Yogaist. Where had she gone, he wondered.

Moore ambled back to his gate to see if she had returned. He saw the young couple occupying his seat and the adjacent seat. Moore's bag was still near the seat, and the woman across was awake and talking on the phone again, while her son slept next to her. Moore scanned the gate to see if the Yogaist was hanging out, but she wasn't. Her bag was still next to Moore's where he had left his as an act of solidarity. It was a brief act of solidarity. Moore walked back and claimed his bag, throwing it over his shoulder, but left hers there. There seemed to be a little activity at the gate counter, and Moore noticed that the snow outside had slowed down. The snow machines were working furiously on the tarmac. *Who knows, perhaps we'll take off after all,* Moore thought. Still, no departure time was posted. Moore turned and decided to stretch his legs a bit.

As Moore walked, he tried to appear as if he were walking to a destination, but he didn't know where he was headed. He kept an avid eye on the crowds gathered throughout the terminal looking for a single individual: a snowflake, he thought. She was stately, look for stately. He walked past one fast-food kiosk after another. He walked past a book and magazine kiosk store. He stepped in and browsed, looking around to see if she might be here. He picked up a golf magazine, flipped through a few pages, and from the vantage point of the shop he lifted his eyes to see if she might be passing by on the concourse—or was she on the other side of the concourse at a different gate providing yoga lessons to some other unsuspecting but stranded businessman?

Jealousy rippled Moore's heart. He felt stupid all of a sudden. How can she be showing someone else yoga? She left her yoga mat by her bag. Then he remembered that she said she was on a pilgrimage and who knows, but perhaps part of her pilgrimage was to walk about the airport and sample the transient group of travelers who were collectively being held together in this long moment of time, but who, once the runways opened up, would never be brought together again—but dispersed out into the world with this moment in time forgotten and lost by all who shared it.

Moore wouldn't forget this moment, though, he thought. Of all the countless airports he had spent time in, of all the crowds—because of the Yogaist and because of that phrase "loving-kindness"—he's pretty sure he would never forget this particular airport layover.

Moore walked past a place serving clam chowder in sourdough bread. Except for a person sitting at the bar and a couple of waitresses milling about, it was one of the few concourse restaurants that was empty, a bad sign for a business serving seafood; nevertheless, Moore couldn't resist clam chowder in a bowl made out of sourdough bread and he sat down at a table facing the passing crowds on the concourse.

When the waitress came, she smiled at Moore in such a way that suggested she was actually happy to see him. Moore knew the look. He was practiced at it himself: that welcoming smile that seemed genuine and what others called midwestern openness was one of Moore's greatest gifts. Hers was a younger face and a gentler more naturally happy smile; his, he worried, had become all too apparently a smiling mask. Her smile was filled with warmth and it made Moore happy and he naturally smiled happily back at her.

What will you have, sir?

Why, I'll have clam chowder in the sourdough bread, of course. How is the chowder?

It was just freshly made by our chef an hour ago, as was our bread. We make everything from scratch and it's all fresh.

That sounds delicious, Moore said. I'll have a blue cheese salad, garlic bread, and the chowder. If I'm still hungry, I may try your key lime pie.

I love our key lime pie, the waitress said. And I'm not just saying that because I work here.

In the meantime, I'll take a cold beer of whatever you have on tap.

Our IPA is from a local brewer.

That sounds perfect.

Moore smiled at her again, and she smiled back at him, then disappeared to place the order.

While Moore sat there the heavy man from his gate walked through the doors. The man stood a moment near the bar looking up at the menu, and then, evidently pleased with the offerings, he decided to sit down. He sat down, of all places, next to Moore. He acknowledged Moore by nodding his head, and as he sat down, he turned to Moore and said,

It's been quite a wait.

Yes, Moore agreed.

Helluva snowstorm out there too.

Yes, Moore agreed again.

I saw you doing yoga with that woman. Do you know her or did she just come up to you?

Moore didn't know how to answer the question, and so he answered it honestly: She just came up to me.

She's a pretty girl, the man said.

Yes.

I reckon we have time enough to eat a bowl of soup and then they'll be moving the planes again, the man said.

Moore asked him: Did they make an announcement?

They did, the man said. They said they're clearing up the runway, and ours should be ready for liftoff in thirty minutes or so.

The waitress showed up with Moore's order. She then took the heavy man's order. The man nodded toward Moore's plate.

I'll have what he's having.

Moore took a sip of the beer.

How's the beer? the gentleman asked.

The beer is good, Moore said.

Sounds good. I'll have a beer too.

The IPA? the waitress confirmed.

Yes. The IPA.

When the waitress left, Moore turned and asked the man where he's from.

Iowa, the man said. Davenport.

What's it like living in Iowa these days? Moore asked.

Funny you should ask that, the heavy man said. It seems if you live in Iowa, whenever you leave Iowa, people always want to know what

182

it's like living in Iowa. But no one who lives in Iowa would ever think to ask that question.

Funny, I grew up on some land just outside Newton.

I know the place, the gentleman said. Where do you live now?

I live in an apartment in Chicago.

And do you find people asking you about what life is like in Chicago?

No, not really. But people still ask me what it was like growing up in Iowa. It's the craziest thing.

Not much to report on, is there? the gentleman asked.

Nope. Not much. And that's what people don't seem to understand.

The two men chuckled and then grew quiet.

What do you do now? the man asked Moore.

Sales, Moore said. I travel a bit. As I say, I live in Chicago. I'm headquartered there. Though for all practical purposes you might say I live in these airports, all the time I spend in them.

You travel a lot? the man asked.

I do, Moore said. I travel all over the country—I'm on the road three hundred days a year.

A traveling salesman!

My territory has grown to cover the entire continental US and parts of Canada. I'm lucky, though, I've not yet made any business contacts in Alaska or Hawaii. Otherwise, I have contacts in every state.

It felt good all of a sudden to be talking to a real human. So much of Moore's time was spent speculating and talking to himself. In his earlier days of travel he used to love to talk to other travelers. There were all sorts of things to be learned talking to strangers. It was interesting to find out so many of them were hardly different from him. Of course Moore also learned that a good many were quite different. A stranger was like a window you could look through to see different parts of the world, that's how Moore used to like to think of it, and now here he was, peering into this gentleman's world. In exchange, the gentleman got to peer into Moore's world.

Sounds like you've gone a long way from small-town Iowa, the gentleman said after a moment.

I've been quite a long way from Iowa, Moore said. After my parents passed, I never had cause to return to the place. I wouldn't go back were it not for a couple of customers I have in Des Moines. How about you? Do you still live in Iowa?

I do, the gentleman said. I always have. My family runs a small pawnshop in town. It's been in the family a few generations. It's kept all of us going for some time.

And how's business nowadays?

Business is good . . . knock wood. With luck, the pawnshop will see me through my own career. When I retire, though, I'll probably end up selling it. Our sons went off to college and they never returned to Iowa.

Where did they go?

One went to Chicago and works as a teacher in a grammar school. Another one is up in Madison. He's a botanist there.

The waitress returned with the gentleman's dinner. Moore watched the man pick up a piece of garlic bread and he rather daintily dipped it into his soup and took a small bite. He munched his food carefully, then took a sip of beer and seemed to follow a thought while he did so.

I just buried my own parents, the gentleman said, which is why I'm here.

They don't live in Iowa?

No. After they sold the pawnshop to me they retired to Rochester, New York, of all places. My mom's people are from up there. Interesting enough, I never knew the Rochester side of the family all that well—they never came to Iowa and we never went to Rochester—but there's a graveyard filled with all sorts of people that have the same last name as my mother. She was laid out next to her twelve siblings.

She was the last to go and she was the youngest by nearly seven years.

The gentleman dipped his bread, then nibbled a portion off it and chewed methodically. He took another sip of beer. He went on talking, almost absent-mindedly.

My mom, she was a love child I guess you'd say, though she didn't have much love for her family as far as I could tell. Don't ask me why. Those in the family that still live in Rochester all came to the funeral, and to be honest it was nice being with them. They're all good people. I hosted a banquet and the whole weekend I kept trying to get to the bottom of what might have caused the rift in the family. They all had nice memories of my mom. As a little girl she won a dance contest sponsored by some old rich lady in New York City, and as a reward this old lady took my mom to Paris to see the Russian Ballet perform Stravinsky's *Rite of Spring*. And can you believe it, I never knew this story of my mom. That was something I learned this weekend.

Some of the oldsters remembered the story—they said Mom was famous in a way, because she was known as the first person in our family to go back to Europe. She was also the first to go to college. She went to Grinnell in Iowa to study dance—that I knew. Once she left Rochester, as far as I can tell, she never had an inclination to go back. She spent most of her life working behind the counter at our pawnshop. You'd never know she'd once been a ballerina if you ever saw her, she was a small portly woman. To think she saw the Russian Ballet in Paris—why, even I'm impressed with that bit of knowledge. I wish I had some memento of hers from that period. I asked around but nothing much remains from that time.

The gentleman took another bite and quietly chewed his morsel. He took a sip of beer. Moore was just about finished with his soup. He finished his beer and ordered another—two beers might possibly help him get some sleep on the plane, should the plane get moving.

You said they were clearing the runway? Moore asked.

Yes, a half hour or so and then I think we might board.

Moore went ahead and ordered the beer. When the waitress returned, Moore smiled at her. The heavy man noticed and smiled at her as well, then went back to his soup.

The thing is, the gentleman continued, when I asked around to see if there was any ill will in the family that would keep my mother away from Rochester most of her life, no one knew. They didn't know why she never came home until late in life. They supposed it only had to do with distance and no one in the family likes to travel. It's genetic, I suppose. I don't much like it myself except in cases of emergency, which under the present conditions—well, you see why I'm stranded here just like you. Funny, if it weren't for burying my mother, I wouldn't be in this airport. Only other time I ever flew on a plane was to Disneyland in California. We took Delta into Anaheim when the boys were small—but that was a long time ago, 1967. Lots of water under the bridge since then, if you know what I mean . . . The man took a sly look at Moore, and Moore shook his head.

I know what you mean, Moore said, flashing one of his customary smiles.

Back then everyone was scared the hippies were going to take over—but they never really did, did they?

Nope, Moore said.

Believe it or not, I was a hippie once, the man continued . . . Those were my glory years. My wife calls it my heyday. She always refers to my hippie years—it was more like just a year—as my heyday. She says, His Heyday. Well I grew my hair not exactly long coming off a flattop and I hitched from Davenport, Iowa, to Little Rock, Arkansas. You know why I went to Little Rock?

No, Moore said.

Because that's where the trucker was headed who picked me up outside of Moline, Iowa. He drove a refrigerated meat truck, pork, and I decided just to hang on for the ride. When I got to Little Rock we made arrangements that he'd pick me up on his return trip a few days later and I took him up on it—he came back to Davenport with Gulf Coast shrimp from Mississippi. I rode in his cab all the

186

way down and all the way back. The one thing that he told me that I'll never forget: by Jupiter. He used that phrase many times he was talking and I never forgot that about him. I've used that phrase most of my life ever since so I suppose you could say that trucker had an impact on me.

Moore was watching the folks pass on the concourse and he had yet to spot the Yogaist. He finished up his beer and thanked the man for the conversation.

I'll see you back on the plane, Moore said.

If it takes off, by Jupiter. Otherwise we'll be sleeping here tonight.

I hope not, Moore said.

Me neither.

chapter 37
nimbostratus praecipitatio

Moore decided to walk the concourse. He walked quickly—big strides—to stretch his legs. The snow had mostly abated outside. Airline staff were repopulating the gates and flight counters and lines were starting to form for check-in and boarding. Travelers were waking up at the gates and they were starting to consolidate their stuff.

The television monitors at the gates continued to blare cable news, talking about something or another—the massive snowstorm crippling travel on the Eastern Seaboard to the Midwest; the endless and unresolved national political strife riving the country; out-of-control forest fires in the West, and the migrations of people up from the south fleeing political unrest and natural disasters creating social upheaval in the southwestern border states. On and on it went.

Moore checked an arrivals board and saw that his plane was now scheduled for a 7:30 p.m. takeoff to Chicago (ORD) with a 10:07 p.m. arrival. He only had a few moments to survey the airport and see if he might discover where his Yogaist had gone. *Surely she can read the arrivals and departures board,* Moore thought, *so she must know that departure is imminent. I wonder where she could be.*

Moore noticed a sign to the airport chapel and on a whim he decided to check it out—it was only a few gates away and a left turn down a different concourse.

In all his years of air travel, Moore had never stopped in to the airport chapel. He had no need to. He wasn't religious, though now it occurs to him that the quiet of a nondenominational sanctuary might actually be a fine place to seek refuge on occasions when he was stranded like this. Who knows what or who he might find in the airport chapel. Was it possible that his Yogaist was in the chapel and she may not realize that the storm outside has abated and now the airport was coming back to life, readying itself to launch all of these stranded travelers back into the skies whence they came, toward home, or to where they are destined away from home.

Entry into the chapel was through a nondescript door. Moore pulled on the door and saw that the chapel was a small interior room with six or seven pews facing a small altar. A votive waxen candle burned on a stand near the altar.

The priest and the old lady who had sat next to the priest at the gate were in the first pew. They sat there quietly saying the rosary together. When Moore stepped into the chapel, the priest looked over his shoulder at Moore and then went back to his ministrations with the older traveler. Moore didn't know whether to interrupt them or not, but he ever so quietly moved to the front of the chapel and in his politest voice he informed the priest and old woman that the plane was departing soon.

Thanks for letting us know, the priest said, in a surprisingly strong voice. One more Glory Be and we should be good to go. The old woman smiled at Moore and thanked him.

Would you like to join us? she asked.

The way she asked it reminded Moore of the way his Yogaist had invited him to join her doing yoga; the sound of her voice was also stronger than he imagined it might be. Who was he to say no to such a woman? And so Moore sat down next to them and joined them in an Our Father, a Hail Mary, and a Glory Be. Moore knew all the words

189

by heart, of course. He'd been an altar boy, after all, though that experience had soured him on religion. This experience, by contrast, was so calming and genteel—he thought it might awaken something in him. But maybe not, he was too busy a guy and he hardly had time in his life to keep his laundry clean and his bills paid.

Shall we be off, Moore said.

We shall, the priest agreed.

Moore helped the lady up. With her hand on the cane and her other hand on the priest's arm they made their way out of the small chapel.

I'm glad you got us, the priest said. I would not have liked to miss our flight after all of this waiting.

Nor would I, the old lady agreed. Moore held the door, and off they went to the gate. On a whim, though, Moore had second thoughts and decided to turn and circle through the concourse one last time to try to catch the Yogaist and inform her that the plane was leaving. He didn't want to leave without her.

Go on ahead, Moore said to the priest. I'll catch up with you guys at the gate. I'll use the last few moments to stretch my legs.

Who am I? What am I?

I am a six, Moore thought.

Crowds of people passed by in both directions. Moore was simultaneously being overtaken and overcome. In the crowd of faces he couldn't identify a single one and yet they all seemed so achingly familiar. Who are you, he wanted to ask: Who are all of you people and how did so many of you come to be stranded at a place like this?

Moore stopped in the middle of the concourse and looked behind him toward his gate. He spun around to look onward in the opposite direction. He swung around again toward his gate and around again and around and slowly he started to twirl in pirouettes. *If I were a ballerina,* he thought, *I'd be in sixth position but there is no sixth position in ballet and yet on this concourse there must be for that is what I am. I am* a numerical iteration lost in a vast chain of numbers. I am a singularity and I am a repeating number in an endless chain, and yet, the rate I'm going, I shall never repeat myself. I am the end of the line. I'm a termination. An end point. A zero.

With that, Moore stopped spinning. He paused to catch his breath. *My oh my*, he said. *I had no idea there were trees like this.* He was dizzy. He stumbled slightly. He heaved and bucked, caught off balance, until his footwork—not dazzling—brought him to a standstill.

He looked around and the crowds continued passing by on both sides; they passed by and not a single person seemed to notice him. How astonishing, Moore thought. A lunatic performance in a crowded airport and yet no one seems to notice, not even security. No one notices because it's not unusual for there to be at least one lunatic in a crowd, or perhaps he was unnoticed because he was invisible and he just didn't matter?

Just then, Moore decided to join the rank and file and to become a number in line at his numbered gate waiting for a numbered seat on a numbered plane to take off in an assigned spot in a long queue of planes taking off into the crepuscular and snowy skies.

Moore turned and walked back—big strides and confident—to his gate. *It's a hollow confidence*, he thought. When he arrived at his gate, to his shock and dismay the bag of his—*of my*, Moore thought, *of my Yogaist*—was gone. A long line had formed for boarding; he searched it for some stately woman and she wasn't to be found. She wasn't to be found either in the line or at the gate. She was gone. And he was alone again, but now he had, absurdly, to contend with the heartbreak of a missed opportunity.

chapter 38
cirrus castellanus

Moore closed his eyes and as he always did nowadays while trying to beat back some dark gathering cloud of stress, he imagined his Woodsman.

Where is my Woodsman? There he is out in the green pasture at the edge of the woods. He has an adze in his hands and he's chopping away at something. Nearby a dog is chewing on a bone. Something he killed, probably.

When Moore showed up at the edge of the forest the Woodsman laughed, You again!

Yes, Moore said.

What are you ready for?

Anything, Moore said. Point the way.

You look like you're ready to run.

I am, Moore said.

Go ahead, then, the Woodsman said. He set his adze down and stood up, brushing his hands together. If you'd like to run—run. Now's the time for running through the woods! We don't live forever.

Nor, by all evidence, do we run forever. Sooner or later the legs or the back give out, then it's spend the rest of our days hobbling around with a cane or stuck in a chair.

Exactly, the Woodsman concurred. Now you're thinking. But why think when you can run? the Woodsman exhorted. Wherever you go, I'll try to keep up with you.

Okay, then follow me, Moore said. He still wore the Woodsman's plaid jacket. The Woodsman wore Moore's Adidas zippy. Moore took off running into the inscrutable wilds. As he ran, that word "inscrutable" seemed to hover just beyond his reach. The faster he ran, the more the word "inscrutable" tantalized him. He thought for a moment that he was a greyhound at the track chasing after the mechanical rabbit. Only in this case the mechanical rabbit was the word "inscrutable." I don't think I have ever used that word before, Moore said, leaping over a log into a bed of ferns that rose nearly up to his waist, shouting as he did so, "Inscrutable!"

The ferns were fragrant and lovely and ancient, and running through them in the shadows of the towering trees made Moore happier than he had ever been before. Moore ran, his chest pushed out in front of him, and his feet moved effortlessly, his knees pumping up and down and the thing is—Moore had no trouble whatsoever breathing. For the first time in his life he ran without the slightest resistance. What joy he felt! He thought of the winged statues of Nike that he had seen. Where had he seen these sculptures? A museum in New York City? Why were these winged sculptures in a museum in the first place? They should be scattered in an ancient wood, like the markers of the vanished civilization that they represented—not housed in some useless museum in the city.

Moore ran after the word "inscrutable," which danced just beyond his reach, and he longed to see popping out of the spongy turf of the forest floor some lichen-etched archaic marble sculptures of a winged Zeus or a Nike or some other Greek deity like sublime Apollo cracked, tilted over, broken and tumbled down by gravity and the slow force of time that seemed to bring everything to its knees, eventually.

Are you running with a purpose? the Woodsman screamed, quick on Moore's heels, or are you just dillydallying? Because if you're just dillydallying, I'll take over the lead and show you how to really run as if you have somewhere to be!

Just then Moore stopped his running and turned to face the Woodsman. They stood in the high ferns. What are you talking about? Moore asked.

If you're just dillydallying, then let me take over the lead, the Woodsman said. I'll show you how to get somewhere!

Moore raised his hand to stop the Woodsman midsentence: But you don't understand, he said. I haven't dillydallied since I was a boy growing up in Iowa. I don't think I've spent a single day of my life since I was a teenager running just randomly through the woods with nowhere in particular to go. All of my subsequent life has been consumed with getting somewhere as the crow flies and as quickly as possible. Can we just trot along, you and I, a little more, with nowhere in particular to go? Can we just enjoy the run, for the run's sake? My oh my, it's beautiful here! How do you learn to live with such beauty?

Believe me, the Woodsman said. It doesn't take much time at all living here hand-to-mouth just scraping by before you forget the beauty and all you see is the difficulty of living another day. In my life, I don't have time to dillydally. Stop for a day or two and before you know it you're so far behind there's no telling how you'll ever catch up again: as if catching up were even possible. Of course I have my dog who depends on me. Let her dillydally while I make sure she has the space and safety to do so.

There was a noise and overhead they saw a bald eagle leave its nest and fly majestically through the trees. The eagle swooped and flew low to the ground and its giant wings were stretched out: flumph, flumph, flumph, the draft of the swooping eagle shook the fern-fronds and up it went. Its golden talons hung low and when Moore saw them hanging thusly, he thought they were sacred talons: the sharpness at the tips of them were to grab the perch still slippery and flapping with life from the water.

194

The great bird flew ahead of Moore, and Moore sought to keep up. He lifted his own arms to follow the eagle and he began pumping his legs in full stride, and the Woodsman, nodding his assent, said, Go ahead, mister! Go! Fly away! If you'd like to follow that eagle, don't let me stop you. Hiyya!

So long, Moore said to the Woodsman. Hiyya!

With that Moore was off running, then flying, up through the towering trees. One wing flap followed another wing flap and the surging draft beneath Moore's wings lifted him. Suddenly Moore was high above ground like the eagle. The great updraft beneath Moore's wings lifted him yet higher. Hiyya! he shouted. This is my transubstantiation! This is how it's done! The wind was steady beneath his wings, it flowed through his wild mane of hair, and up, up he went toward the towering snow-capped mountaintops and to the inscrutable white cirrus castellanus cloud formation beyond that formed and re-formed themselves into the likeness of everyone whom he had ever known and loved.

chapter 39
nimbostratus virga

As the plane lifted off the tarmac, Moore was pulled by the force of the plane into the back of his seat. This light load of g-force was a familiar sensation. The first time Moore had ever flown on a plane it had tickled his insides and it made him laugh. Ever since, he had sought but could not find that same tickling sensation.

Nevertheless, Moore felt grateful for this gift of flight. It was amazing to him, that this whole thing—air travel—was even possible at all: the bravery of pilots flying huge aircraft into the skies as easily as if they were driving the common city bus through the streets, and all of the organization and preparation that goes into each flight—it must take an army, and Moore knew that it did. There were millions of people working in relation to the airline industry, and every one of them, in their own way, was dedicated to this miraculous feat of sending several hundred people at a time airborne, miles above Earth, in a reasonably timely and safe manner toward home or some other destination.

In his case, Moore was headed home. *In a few hours, I will be landing. The plane will taxi a bit, hopefully we'll be granted a terminal, then we'll dock and the sound of a beep and the steward of the plane will announce:* You are now safe to unfasten your seat belt. Please use caution when opening overhead luggage bins as some contents may have shifted during flight. It is currently twenty-eight degrees and snowy in Chicago. Local time is one o'clock a.m. Please enjoy your stay in Chicago, and on behalf of United Airlines and all of its employees we thank you for flying with us today. *And this announcement will be followed by the first few bars of Gershwin's "Rhapsody in Blue."* The melody flowed into Moore's brain now as an advertising jingle.

It was too bad, Moore thought, even as he hummed along to Gershwin's melody. It was too bad the way these huge corporate enterprises were able to co-opt and trademark the language—not to mention popular culture both low and high—for their own advertising purposes. Why, just look at what they did to George Gershwin's tune "Rhapsody in Blue," cycling it around into an advertising jingle so that you no longer heard the music or what meaning it claimed on its own lyric powers. Instead you saw aircraft taking off and landing, what a shame.

As a child living in Iowa, Moore had a cassette recording of that piece along with Gershwin's "An American in Paris" played by Leonard Bernstein and the New York Philharmonic. Listening to Gershwin's music with Bernstein at the helm of the orchestra made Moore feel slightly less than provincial. He listened to it in the dark of his small room, the moon outside casting a lonesome light through his window shade, the cricket-chirr and toad-trilling providing the appropriate background noise.

Gershwin's music helped Moore imagine places far beyond his room and this tiny place he had grown up in on a small farm in Iowa. All his life Moore wished he could be like a bird and fly away from this place. He felt jealous of the birds that did fly away—*they don't even have sense enough to know where they fly to or what they're flying from, but I would. I would have sense enough to appreciate any place other than this one.*

When the highway had been built through his childhood town, Moore had spent many evenings fascinated, peering over the guardrail of the bridge, watching the interstate and all those countless people rushing by beneath him as if they had some other better

197

place to be than here. Later in life, when Moore landed this job with Sonnenshein & Sons and he learned of the travel that would be involved—something leaped in his heart not unlike that tickling sensation he felt when he first took off for flight in a plane.

In a weird way, it was something Moore had always dreamed of doing. He had always wanted to be on the go. As a boy standing over the highway, Moore had hoped to have a busy career that took him places. He had wanted to bounce around from place to place. Moore discovered in the process of all these long years on the road that not only was he suited for travel, but he was a good salesman as well. This last part surprised him. Moore never expected to be good at anything, and yet here was the proof: he outsold all of his colleagues considerably. He was the pillar upon which the greatest hope for company gain was placed, and just the other day, Harvey Sonnenshein, afraid he might lose his great prodigal, had just proposed that if Moore hit his targets by the end of the fiscal year he would up Moore to 150 percent of his target bonus.

Moore was always advising and mentoring his colleagues and his advice was appreciated. He well knew what products were best suited for the marketplace. He knew, of course, because he had daily encounters with the unforgiving marketplace. He covered the four corners of it. *I understand it*, Moore thought, *because I live it*.

Moore was tired now. He looked across the aisle of the plane and he saw, in the same row as him, that woman who had spent most of the evening chattering madly, insanely on the phone, with her gorgon of curls and that long straining neck, and her son was by her side. It made Moore happy just to look at her and her son and he supposed that the sight of them was some consolation for the loss of his Yogaist. *At least she, with her child, is still in view—they haven't abandoned me yet.*

Her face would likely linger in Moore's mind, giving him something to dream about as he drifted off to sleep in the snug comfort of his own bed. Too bad, he thought, about that Yogaist—that she had fled him. Would he ever encounter her again? Unlikely.

Wasn't it the way? Moore wondered. He always seemed to be coming close but never able to close on relationships. He was a wonderful salesman when it came to selling his product but he was all too fallibly human when it came to selling his own prospects to another.

The woman's son had his head in her lap. His electronic game lay between them, and she ran her fingers through his hair and gently stroked his cheek with the tips of her fingernails. What was her name? Moore wondered. He wished he had a name to attach to such a lovely visage. He thought of the name Emily. Moore loved the name Emily. He always had. He secretly felt that the woman he met one day would be named Emily. It was a hunch, but a deep-seated one, which he was unable to shake. He'd give the woman with the gorgon curls that name now, just for the heck of it: "Emily."

As Moore peered over admiring her, he saw in the window that she leaned against his own reflection. Moore was gazing intently, and there it was, his own face smiling back at him. It was as if Emily were leaning against his ghostly self, and for a moment, Moore felt he belonged to the closed circle of her family universe. *That's what I want. More than anything in the world, I want a small family of my own to harbor me.* Why was it so difficult to obtain?

A moment later, Emily pulled down the shade; she turned off her overhead lamp and her body twisted away from Moore as she attempted to get comfortable for a few hours' sleep on the darkened plane.

Moore would stay awake the whole flight home, no matter how tired he was. He had a hard time sleeping on planes. It made his job harder than it should otherwise be. If he could only sleep on these birds, his job would be considerably easier. As it was, he would contend with his own thoughts through the night, weighing doubt against doubt, sadness against sadness.

I'm not sad or doubtful, only curious when a change will occur. When will it happen that I'll be found and discovered and liberated from myself?

Moore would land in Chicago (ORD) in a few hours. In thirty-six hours he'd be off again, headed who knows where: was it Cleveland

(CLE) or Fargo (FAR)? He couldn't say . . . He'd have to check his schedule, though his gut told him it was Fargo. Didn't that say it all? Moore wondered. Wasn't that the crux of the matter: Fargo. Go far. Be far. Be gone. And Home, which was always somewhere else, beckoned. No, it didn't beckon. It tugged at his heart.